Memories of The Highlands Trilogy

THE WHISPERING HILLS

Book 1

By Morgan DeSpiegelaere

i

Disclaimer

This is a work of fiction. All characters, places, and events depicted in this novel are products of the author's imagination. Any resemblance to real persons, living or dead, or actual events is purely coincidental. The locations, names, and circumstances within this story have been crafted for the sole purpose of the narrative and are not based on real-world counterparts.

Dedication

To those who believe in the magic of the universe, the power of love, and the what guides us forward. This story is for you, who find beauty in the untold and strength in the unknown.

And to the dreamers — may you always chase the shadows of your heart.

Acknowledgments

To my family and friends — thank you for your endless support, encouragement, and belief in my stories, even on the days when doubt crept in. Your love and patience fuel my passion to write.

To my readers — your love of stories, your connection to these characters, and your unwavering support mean more to me than words can express. This book exists because of you, and I'm endlessly grateful for your kind hearts and your trust in my work.

And finally, to my dreams — the ones that keep me awake at night, pushing me to tell stories that linger in the hearts of others. You are my guiding stars.

Prologue

The dream came again.

It always began the same way—mist curling around her bare ankles, the scent of rain on wild heather thick in the air. The wind whispered through the hills, soft as a lover's breath against her skin, carrying a name she could never quite grasp.

Somewhere in the distance, water lapped against stone, steady and rhythmic. A loch? A river? She wasn't sure. All she knew was the pull—the irresistible ache to step forward, to chase the shadow slipping between the trees just ahead.

She could hear him.

Not a voice, but a presence. A feeling.

Heat.

The air thickened, charged with something electric, something primal. Her breath hitched as unseen hands traced her waist, a touch so real it stole the air from her lungs. A breath ghosted along her throat, and she shivered as lips — warm, demanding — pressed to the delicate skin just below her ear.

"You are mine".

A tremor rippled through her, a sensation both foreign and familiar, laced with a longing that should not exist.

She turned.

And he was there.

Tall. Broad. Power coiled beneath the surface of his body, all lean muscle and restrained strength. His hair, dark as a raven's wing, tumbled past his shoulders, damp with rain. His jaw was sharp, dusted with the barest hint of stubble, like he hadn't shaved in days. He looked wild—untamed.

But it was his eyes that stole her breath.

A piercing, soul-deep blue, burning like the edge of a storm just before it breaks. Shadows and fire lived in those depths, something ancient, something waiting.

His gaze raked over her, unreadable, intense, like he was trying to memorize every inch of her. His lips—full, devastating—parted slightly, and she swore she could taste him on the air, something dark and sweet, whiskey and rain.

Evelyn's pulse hammered.

She knew this man. She knew him.

But how?

His hand lifted to gently caress her face, his fingers trailing through the soft waves of her long, curly brown hair. The faintest brush of his fingertips against her wrist sent a rush of warmth flooding through her, as though igniting a spark deep within her. Her breath caught, her chest tightening as his grip deepened, holding her in place with a tenderness that felt like a promise, ensuring she couldn't escape.

"Who are you?" she whispered.

A flash—

Lightning split the sky, illuminating the world in a blinding silver glow.

For a heartbeat, everything was too sharp.

The fierce cut of his cheekbones.

The unreadable intensity in his gaze.

And behind him —

An old wooden sign, worn with time, the letters barely visible beneath layers of moss and age.

Glen Torrin.

The name punched through her like a breath stolen from her lungs.

A gasp, a name torn from her lips —

And then —

She woke.

The wind clawed at her shutters, rattling the glass panes of Evelyn Sinclair's small flat. The city hummed around her, cold and unfamiliar, but the heat lingered on her skin, the scent of rain and heather still clinging to her senses.

Glen Torrin.

She had never been there.

Chapter 1: The Restless Heart

The sky over London was the color of wet concrete, a dull, suffocating grey that stretched endlessly overhead. The streets below bustled with the familiar chaos of a weekday morning—heels clicking against pavement, the drone of engines, and the occasional bark of a street vendor shouting over the rush.

Inside the towering glass building of Campbell & Whitmore Financial, Evelyn Sinclair sat at her desk, staring at the blinking cursor on her computer screen. The report she was meant to finish had been open for an hour, yet she hadn't typed more than a few sentences.

She rubbed her temple, exhaling slowly.

The office was as stifling as ever, its artificial light humming faintly above her. The air smelled of stale coffee and cheap printer ink, the scent clinging to the beige walls and grey cubicles, as if it had soaked into the very fabric of the building. The monotony of it all made her chest tighten.

Her eyes flickered to the digital clock in the corner of her screen. 10:07 AM.

Only two more hours until lunch. Seven more until she could leave.

Was this what life was meant to be? Counting down the hours until she could be somewhere else?

Her desk was as uninspiring as the rest of the office — neatly arranged papers, a company-issued notebook, and a potted plant no bigger than her palm. A gift from her grandmother. It was supposed to be an easy-to-care-for plant, yet its leaves had begun to yellow, wilting from neglect.

Much like herself, she thought bitterly.

A notification flashed on her screen.

Meeting with Helen – 2:00 PM.

Evelyn's stomach twisted. Helen Westwood, her manager, was not unkind, but she had a way of making every conversation feel like a subtle reprimand.

She could already hear her voice — calm, professional, always tinged with that polite concern that made Evelyn's skin crawl.

"Evelyn, your work has been steady. But we need to see more initiative. More drive. More passion."

Passion.

She almost laughed at the word.

Passion had no place here, buried under spreadsheets and profit margins. She had once been full of it, though. As a child, she had spent hours poring over travel books, running her fingers over glossy images of rolling hills, cobblestone streets, and ancient ruins.

She had dreamed of adventure.

Yet, at thirty years old, she had never stepped foot beyond England's borders.

Her phone buzzed, dragging her from her thoughts.

A message from her mother.

Mum: Don't forget dinner Sunday. Your father wants to talk about your career again.

Evelyn's jaw tightened.

Of course he did.

She could already picture it—her father, sitting at the head of the table, knife and fork poised in his usual no-nonsense manner. "Evelyn, you're not twenty anymore. It's time to be practical. You need to think about your future. Promotions. Buying a home. Stability."

Her mother would nod in agreement, offering her a sympathetic smile but never contradicting him.

Evelyn locked her phone and shoved it into the drawer.

She didn't want to have that conversation.

She didn't want to think about promotions or buying a flat or stability.

She wanted to feel something real.

She leaned back in her chair, staring at the ceiling. Somewhere outside, beyond the steel and glass of this office, beyond the endless deadlines and expectations, the world was waiting.

She had spent so many years waiting for the right moment to leave. But what if the right moment never came?

What if she was still here in five years? Ten?

A sudden, sharp ache formed in her chest.

She glanced at the framed photo on her desk — her grandmother, a warm smile on her lined face, standing in front of a sprawling green hillside.

Scotland.

Her grandmother had spoken of it often, her voice soft with longing.

"There's magic in the Highlands, Evie," she had said. "The kind that speaks to your soul."

Evelyn had always promised herself she would go one day.

But "one day" had turned into years.

And she was still here.

Her fingers hovered over her keyboard, but instead of typing her report, she hesitated. A quiet whisper stirred at the edges of her mind. A restless feeling she couldn't quite name.

What if she actually did it?

What if she just… went?

The thought sent a shiver down her spine.

It was ridiculous. Irresponsible. Impossible.

Wasn't it?

Her heart pounded.

And yet, for the first time in a long time, she felt something other than exhaustion.

She felt alive.

And that terrified her.

Chapter 2: The Call to Adventure

The rain had started sometime in the afternoon, a steady, relentless drizzle that coated the streets in a sheen of silver. The faint patter against the office window was the only sound Evelyn could focus on as she sat across from Helen Westwood, her manager.

Helen's office was pristine, much like the woman herself — modern, efficient, completely devoid of warmth. The only personal touch was a single framed photograph on the desk, a corporate event where Helen stood, arms folded, in front of a banner that read: "Leadership. Performance. Growth."

Evelyn forced herself to sit upright, hands folded neatly in her lap.

Helen sighed and leaned forward, her manicured fingers tapping against the desk. "Evelyn, I won't sugarcoat this. You're… steady. Reliable. But we need more from you."

There it was. The same speech Evelyn had heard a dozen times.

"I understand," she said, keeping her voice even.

Helen raised a brow. "Do you? Because your recent reports have been adequate, but there's no initiative. No long-term vision. You've been with the company for seven years. Don't you want to move up?"

No.

She should. She knew that. Everyone else in her department was scrambling for promotions, for raises, for the next step up the corporate ladder. But Evelyn couldn't summon even an ounce of desire for it.

She forced a tight-lipped smile. "Of course."

Helen exhaled, looking unimpressed. "Look, Evelyn, I don't want to push you, but you're not fresh out of university anymore. It's time to start thinking about your future."

The words echoed her father so perfectly that Evelyn's throat tightened.

She nodded, murmured something polite, and escaped the office as soon as she could.

By the time Evelyn reached her flat, the rain had turned to mist, clinging to the windows like a breathy whisper.

Her one-bedroom apartment was tidy but impersonal — books stacked in neat piles, a few framed photographs on the shelf, a couch that had seen better days. It was a space designed for someone who never quite settled.

She shrugged off her coat, tossing it onto the chair before padding toward the kitchen. A cup of tea. That's what she needed. Something warm. Something grounding.

But as she reached for the kettle, her gaze caught on a small wooden box tucked on the shelf above the counter.

Her grandmother's box.

Evelyn hesitated, then slowly pulled it down.

It was old, the wood slightly worn, the brass clasp tarnished. Her grandmother had given it to her years ago, filled with trinkets, postcards, and little handwritten notes from her travels.

She had never opened it since her passing.

Evelyn swallowed hard and lifted the lid.

Inside, everything was just as she remembered. A bundle of photographs — her grandmother, younger, smiling in front of a loch, standing atop a windswept hill, wrapped in a thick woolen scarf. Postcards with faded ink, maps with edges softened by time.

And at the very bottom, a letter.

Her breath caught.

She recognized the handwriting instantly.

Her grandmother's looping, elegant script.

With trembling fingers, she unfolded the paper.

My Dearest Evie,

By the time you read this, I imagine you've grown into a remarkable woman. I hope you've found adventure, that you've seen the world the way you always dreamed of.

But if you haven't—if you're still waiting—then I need you to hear me.

Go.

Do not wait for the perfect moment. Do not let fear keep you in one place.

Scotland is calling you, my love.

The Highlands whispered to me once, and they are whispering to you now.

Go to the hills. Go and find what is waiting for you.

With love, always,

Grandmother

Evelyn read the words over and over, her heart pounding.

She could almost hear her grandmother's voice, the soft lilt of her accent, the warmth in her tone.

Scotland is calling you.

Her fingers curled around the paper.

A lifetime of hesitation, of waiting for the right time, of letting fear dictate her choices—it all pressed against her like a weight on her chest.

What if, for once in her life, she stopped waiting?

Her pulse quickened.

Before she could talk herself out of it, she grabbed her laptop, her fingers flying across the keyboard.

Flights to Scotland.

The search results loaded. A direct flight to Inverness. Two days from now.

Her hands trembled as she clicked through the booking options.

And then—

A deep breath.

A single click.

Confirmed.

Evelyn exhaled sharply, her heart hammering.

No turning back now.

For the first time in years, she wasn't waiting.

She was going.

Evelyn spent the next day in a daze. At work, she walked through meetings and deadlines like a ghost, nodding at the right moments, pretending to care. But beneath it all, a current of excitement ran through her.

She hadn't told anyone. Not her parents, not Helen, not even her closest friends.

This was hers.

That evening, she pulled an old suitcase from the back of her closet, the same one she had always told herself she'd use someday.

Someday was now.

Folding clothes, tucking in scarves, slipping a journal into the side pocket—every movement felt surreal. She hesitated when she reached her grandmother's wooden box, then carefully placed it inside.

The letter would come with her.

She checked her phone.

One missed call from her mother. Three unread emails from work.

She ignored them all.

Tomorrow, she would wake up in London.

The day after that—

Scotland.

As she lay in bed that night, staring at the ceiling, the whisper of her grandmother's words echoed in her mind.

"The Highlands whispered to me once, and they are whispering to you now."

And for the first time in as long as she could remember—

She listened.

Chapter 3: The Flight to the Unknown

The morning of Evelyn's departure arrived cloaked in a damp London chill. The air smelled of rain-soaked pavement and the lingering scent of coffee from the café beneath her flat. The city hummed with its usual rhythm—buses rumbling past, hurried footsteps on the sidewalk, muffled conversations blending into the morning air.

But today, it all felt different.

Evelyn stood by her suitcase, staring at it as if it held all the answers she had been searching for. The small wooden box containing her grandmother's letter was safely tucked inside, nestled between soft sweaters and scarves meant for the Highland air.

Was she really doing this?

A nervous flutter twisted in her stomach.

She had always imagined this moment would feel exhilarating — liberating. But instead, it was a war between excitement and fear, a constant push and pull inside her chest.

Her phone buzzed on the kitchen counter.

A message from her mother.

Mum: Are you coming for dinner tonight? Dad wants to talk.

Evelyn hesitated, staring at the screen.

She could already picture the scene — her father sitting at the head of the table, wine glass in hand, his expression expectant. He would launch into a speech about responsibility, about career advancement, about why she was wasting her potential.

She exhaled, her fingers tightening around the phone.

This was the moment. The line in the sand.

For years, she had lived for other people's expectations.

Not anymore.

She took a deep breath and typed out a reply.

Me: I can't. I'm going to Scotland.

She hesitated for only a moment before pressing send.

Seconds later, her phone rang.

She let it go to voicemail.

Turning away, she grabbed her suitcase, slung her bag over her shoulder, and stepped out the door.

No more second-guessing. No more waiting.

It was time.

Heathrow buzzed with movement—families with overstuffed suitcases, businessmen scrolling through emails, tourists snapping last-minute photos before heading home. The steady hum of conversations and the occasional overhead announcement created a symphony of controlled chaos.

Evelyn stood in line at the check-in counter, her fingers gripping the handle of her suitcase.

She had flown before, but never like this. Never without a strict itinerary, a return date, a carefully planned list of what to expect.

This was different.

There was no return flight.

No plan beyond landing in Inverness.

Just a deep, unshakable feeling pulling her forward.

The airline attendant smiled politely as she took Evelyn's passport. "Traveling alone?"

Evelyn hesitated before nodding. "Yes."

The word felt strange on her tongue.

She had never truly traveled alone before. Never stepped into the unknown without a safety net.

But maybe that was the point.

After checking in, she made her way through security, her heart hammering as she placed her belongings on the conveyor belt. Everything felt surreal, as if she were floating outside her own body, watching someone else take this risk.

As she walked through the terminal, she spotted a bookstore and instinctively stepped inside.

The scent of paper and ink wrapped around her, grounding her for a moment. She traced her fingers along the spines of travel books, their glossy covers showcasing exotic locations—Rome, Paris, Santorini. But it was the small, worn section on Scotland that caught her eye.

She pulled a book from the shelf. The Mystical Highlands: Legends and Lore.

Flipping through the pages, she found herself captivated by the old stories—whispering hills, ghostly apparitions, ancient ruins that held secrets buried beneath time.

Her grandmother had always spoken of Scotland as if it were more than just a place.

As if it were alive.

She bought the book without hesitation and slipped it into her bag.

A voice crackled over the intercom.

"Now boarding: Flight 218 to Inverness."

Her pulse quickened.

This was it.

Evelyn settled into her window seat, exhaling as she fastened her seatbelt. The plane was smaller than she expected, the hum of engines vibrating beneath her feet.

Outside, the tarmac was slick with rain, reflecting the flashing runway lights.

She was about to leave London behind.

The thought sent a shiver down her spine.

Just as she reached for the in-flight magazine, the seat beside her was suddenly occupied.

A man.

Tall with light brown hair that curled slightly at the ends, and green eyes. He wore a thick sweater, the kind suited for the chill of the north, and carried the faint scent of leather and pine.

"Looks like we're seatmates," he said with an easy grin, his accent distinctly Scottish.

Evelyn managed a polite smile. "Looks like it."

He extended a hand. "Callum."

She hesitated before shaking it. His palm was warm, his grip firm but not overbearing.

"Evelyn."

He tilted his head slightly. "English?"

"Guilty."

Callum chuckled. "And heading to the Highlands, I see. Holiday?"

Evelyn opened her mouth, then closed it.

How did she even begin to explain?

"I… suppose you could call it that," she said finally.

Callum studied her for a moment, as if sensing there was more to the story. But instead of pressing, he simply leaned back. "You picked a good time to visit. Autumn in the Highlands is something else."

Evelyn glanced down at the book in her lap, the one she had bought just before boarding. The words Legends and Lore stared back at her.

Her grandmother's voice echoed in her mind.

"The Highlands whispered to me once, and they are whispering to you now."

She had no idea what awaited her in Scotland.

But as the plane took off, lifting her away from everything she had ever known, she couldn't shake the feeling that she was finally — finally —

heading exactly where she was meant
to be.

Chapter 4: Arrival in the Highlands

The flight had been smooth, but as the plane descended through thick, rolling clouds, Evelyn's heart pounded against her ribs. She pressed her forehead against the window, eyes widening as she caught her first glimpse of Scotland.

A vast, untamed landscape stretched beneath her—deep green hills blanketed in mist, winding rivers cutting through valleys, and lochs shimmering under the overcast sky. The rugged beauty of it stole her breath.

Something stirred in her chest.

A whisper.

Not a sound, not words—just a feeling.

A calling.

She swallowed hard. It had been years since she'd last felt anything so inexplicably right.

Callum, her seatmate, leaned over slightly, glancing at the view. "Not bad, huh?" he murmured.

Evelyn nodded, unable to tear her gaze away. "It's... breathtaking."

He chuckled. "Aye, that it is. But it's better down there. The air, the quiet—it gets in your bones."

She shivered.

The plane landed with a gentle bounce, rolling down the tarmac before slowing to a halt.

The intercom crackled. **"Welcome to Inverness."**

This was it.

No turning back.

The airport was small, a stark contrast to the sprawling chaos of Heathrow. As Evelyn stepped off the plane, the cool Highland air rushed to greet her, crisp and pure, tinged with the scent of damp earth and distant pine.

She inhaled deeply, filling her lungs.

Freedom.

She had never felt it like this before.

Inside, the terminal was quiet, passengers dispersing quickly. She retrieved her suitcase and checked her phone. No messages from her mother — not yet. But she knew they would come.

Now, she had a journey to begin.

She walked through the sliding doors, stepping fully into Scotland for the first time.

And then—

A gust of wind curled around her, brushing against her cheek like a whispering hand.

She froze.

It wasn't just the wind. It was… something else.

A feeling. A presence.

The hairs on the back of her neck stood up.

Was she imagining it?

"Lost already?"

She jumped slightly, turning to find Callum beside her, his hands tucked into his coat pockets.

"I—no," she stammered, regaining her composure. "I just…" She hesitated. "I thought I felt something."

Callum arched an eyebrow, his expression amused but not dismissive. "Aye. That happens here."

Her brow furrowed. "What do you mean?"

He shrugged. "Some say the Highlands have a soul of their own. That they whisper to those who are meant to be here."

Evelyn's heart thudded.

She didn't respond.

She couldn't.

Because deep down, she knew—

That was exactly what she had felt.

Evelyn had rented a car, a small silver hatchback that seemed almost laughable against the rugged landscape. As she drove out of Inverness, the city quickly faded behind her, replaced by open roads that wound through towering mountains and sweeping moors.

The further she went, the wilder it became.

The hills rose like ancient guardians, their peaks vanishing into mist. Sheep dotted the fields, unbothered by the occasional passing car. Streams cut through the land like silver veins, and the sky stretched vast and endless overhead.

She had seen pictures.

Nothing compared to this.

The road narrowed as she entered deeper into the Highlands, the silence pressing in. No billboards. No traffic. Just the whisper of wind through the glens.

She pulled over at a small lookout point, stepping out of the car. The air was colder here, carrying the scent of heather and damp stone.

And then—

She heard it.

A whisper.

Soft. Faint. Almost lost to the wind.

Her breath caught.

She turned slowly, scanning the empty hills.

Nothing.

And yet…

The feeling was there. Stronger than before.

She closed her eyes, letting it wash over her.

She wasn't alone.

Not in a physical sense — there was no one nearby.

But the land itself —

It was alive.

Evelyn pressed a hand to her chest, her heart hammering.

What was happening to her?

As she climbed back into the car, her hands trembled slightly. She wasn't scared. Not exactly.

But something inside her was shifting.

She drove on, the mist thickening as she wound deeper into the Highlands. Her destination was a small inn just outside a village called Glenfinnan, nestled near the shores of Loch Shiel.

The fog grew dense, curling along the road like ghostly fingers.

She slowed the car.

And then—

A figure appeared in the mist.

A man.

He was walking along the side of the road, moving with a steady grace that seemed almost otherworldly, his dark coat trailing behind him. His dark hair was tousled by the wind, and the faintest trace of a beard lined his jaw.

Evelyn's breath caught in her throat.

She couldn't explain it. She couldn't put it into words, but the sight of him, standing there in the mist, made her heart beat faster.

She didn't stop the car. She couldn't.

Her foot instinctively pressed harder on the accelerator, but as she drove past, her eyes locked with his.

A moment.

A single heartbeat.

His eyes—deep, intense as the mist itself—met hers, and Evelyn felt a jolt in her chest, as if the very air between them had charged with some unseen force.

It was a feeling she couldn't ignore.

It wasn't just attraction. It was something… more.

Something ancient.

A pull. A connection.

Her hands gripped the steering wheel tightly, but she couldn't look away.

She passed him.

The mist closed in around her, and as quickly as he had appeared, he was gone, swallowed by the fog.

Evelyn's heart raced, her body trembling as she fought to make sense of what had just happened.

Who was he?

Why did she feel like she knew him?

Her foot eased off the pedal, the road stretching before her like an endless ribbon of mystery.

The mist parted again, but the feeling — the pull — lingered, tightening around her chest like an invisible thread.

Chapter 5: The Call of the Highlands

The engine purred as Evelyn was whirling with her thoughts in the car, her fingers gripping the steering wheel. Her breath came in shallow gasps, her pulse hammering against her ribs. The mist outside swirled in eerie silence, curling like ghostly tendrils around the roadside.

Who was that man?

And why did he elicit such feelings within her?

A tremor ran through her fingers as she forced herself to exhale.

The Highlands weren't just whispering anymore. They were speaking.

By the time she reached the inn in Glenfinnan, night had fallen. The building loomed against the backdrop of the moors, its stone walls thick with moss, its windows glowing dimly in the darkness. It was old—centuries old, if she had to guess—but well-kept, with climbing ivy snaking up the front.

Evelyn stepped inside, the warmth of the interior wrapping around her like a heavy quilt. The scent of burning peat and aged wood filled the air. A fire crackled in the hearth, its flickering light casting long shadows against the wooden beams above.

A woman stood behind the counter, her gray-streaked hair pulled into a loose braid. Her sharp, knowing eyes met Evelyn's with an unsettling familiarity.

"You must be Miss Sinclair," the woman said before Evelyn could even introduce herself.

Evelyn hesitated. "How did you—?"

"It's a small village. Word travels," the woman interrupted, offering a small, enigmatic smile. "I'm Moira. Welcome to the Glenfinnan Inn."

Evelyn forced a polite smile, but something about the woman's gaze unsettled her. She felt observed, almost as if Moira was expecting her.

Later that night, Evelyn lay awake in her room, listening to the wind howl through the hills. Sleep eluded her. The day had been too strange, the air too heavy with something she couldn't name.

She rolled over, trying to push the events from her mind, when she heard it.

A whisper.

Her name.

"Evelyn..."

Her blood ran cold. She bolted upright, eyes scanning the room. The window was open just a crack, the curtains shifting in the breeze. The mist pressed against the glass, thick and unmoving.

She swallowed hard, heart thundering in her chest. Had she really heard it?

Then—

A shadow flickered beyond the mist.

A shape.

A man.

The same man from the road.

Evelyn's breath caught in her throat. She scrambled out of bed, moving to the window, but as soon as she reached it, the mist seemed to pulse, shifting and swallowing the figure whole.

Gone.

The whisper had vanished too, leaving only the sound of the wind.

Evelyn's hands trembled against the windowsill. She knew now —

It wasn't just whispering.

It was calling her by name.

Chapter 6: The Stranger in the Mist

The morning air was damp, carrying the scent of wet earth and heather as Evelyn Sinclair stepped outside the inn. The mist still clung to the hills, weaving through the landscape like a restless spirit, obscuring the path ahead. The night's whispers still echoed in her mind, chilling her more than the crisp Highland air.

Moira had been waiting for her in the common room, a knowing glance passing between them as Evelyn had gathered her things. The innkeeper said nothing but slid a cup of steaming tea toward her, offering a silent comfort Evelyn wasn't yet ready to accept.

She needed answers.

Her hands tightened around the strap of her satchel as she took a tentative step forward. She didn't know where she was going — only that the hills were calling her, drawing her deeper into their folds.

Evelyn's boots crunched against the ground as she wandered through the streets, each step heavy with uncertainty. The town was quiet — too quiet — but there was something about it that tugged at the edges of her memory. The cobblestone paths seemed worn but familiar, the buildings leaning as though tired from years of standing against the wind.

She paused at the crossroads, the air thick with an odd sense of déjà vu. Something about the old stone well at the corner, the crooked lantern post near the square—she had seen them before, in her dreams. Her heart quickened as she took another step, compelled by a pull she couldn't explain. She turned down a forgotten alley, the streetlights dimming as if they hadn't been lit in years. There, half-hidden by vines, moss, and overgrown ivy, stood an old wooden sign. The paint had long since chipped away, but the outline was unmistakable.

Glen Torrin.

Her breath caught in her throat, her mind racing. This was the sign from her dream—the one she had tried to dismiss as a mere figment of her imagination. Yet here it was, in the middle of a forgotten part of town, waiting for her.

A shiver danced down her spine, and she wrapped her arms around herself as if to ward off the sensation. It wasn't fear. It was something deeper. Something unknown.

Then—

A presence.

A shadow shifted in her peripheral vision. A figure stepped into the dim light of the square, and the moment her gaze landed on him, it was as if the world had been knocked off its axis.

Heat. Desire. A crackling intensity surged through her, leaving her breathless.

Tall, broad-shouldered, his frame cut against the mist like something carved from legend. His hair, dark as soot, fell past his shoulders, framing a strong, chiseled face. And his eyes— piercing blue, sharp and full of unrelenting intensity — seared through her, stripping her bare.

Evelyn's heart pounded as recognition slammed into her with the force of a storm. It was him. The man from the road. But more than that —

The man from her dream.

The same dream she'd had over and over again, for as long as she could remember. Always just out of reach. Always a shadow in the mist.

And now he was here, in front of her, as real as the stones beneath her feet.

His gaze locked onto hers, and she swore she saw something flicker there — an echo of recognition. As if he, too, had seen her before. As if she wasn't the only one experiencing this undeniable force between them.

Evelyn's pulse roared in her ears. Her body betrayed her, drawn to him in a way that defied logic, defied reason. Every inch of her skin hummed with an awareness she couldn't understand. As if she had spent a lifetime searching for something she hadn't even known she was missing—until now.

The silence stretched between them, thick with unspoken words, with an electricity that neither of them could ignore.

Finally, he spoke, his voice low, rough, edged with something unreadable. "You feel it too, don't you?"

Evelyn's lips parted, but words failed her. She could only nod.

She shivered—not from cold, but from the otherworldly desire that seeped into her bones, settling deep within her like an undeniable force.

The man exhaled sharply, almost amused, before dipping his head in a half-bow. "Lachlan MacKenzie."

His name settled in the air between them, heavy with unspoken weight.

The name fit him — strong, undeniably Scottish.

Evelyn hesitated, then lifted her chin. "Evelyn Sinclair."

Something flickered across Lachlan's face — recognition, or perhaps something deeper. His gaze shifted, scanning her face as though searching for a memory.

"You shouldn't be wandering alone," he finally said, his voice quieter now. "Not here."

Evelyn's pulse quickened. "Why?"

Lachlan hesitated, glancing toward the mist-covered hills. "Because the past does not sleep in these lands, Miss Sinclair. And you... you have awoken something."

A chill ran down Evelyn's spine, but she forced herself to hold his gaze. "Then tell me what I've woken."

Lachlan studied her for a long moment before sighing, his expression shifting to something more measured. "You're not the first to hear the whispers. But if you truly want to understand, you need to hear the full story." He motioned toward a narrow trail leading away from the inn. "We can talk as we walk, stay within sight of the village, if that makes you feel safer."

Evelyn hesitated, weighing her options. Everything about this was strange, but Lachlan's stance was open, his voice steady. She could turn away now and leave the mystery unsolved, or she could take the first step toward understanding what had been calling her here.

Slowly, cautiously, she nodded. "Alright. Lead the way."

Fate had led her here. And now, she knew with certainty —

This was only the beginning.

Chapter 7: Whispers of the Past

The narrow path wound through the hills, flanked by towering ferns and clusters of wildflowers bent low from the morning dew. The mist still clung stubbornly to the ground, swirling around Evelyn's boots with each cautious step she took. Lachlan MacKenzie walked beside her, his strides unhurried, his hands tucked into the folds of his cloak.

For several moments, silence stretched between them, broken only by the distant call of a curlew. Evelyn found herself stealing glances at him, taking in the sharp cut of his jaw, the way his dark hair curled slightly at the bottom. There was something undeniably rugged about him, something that felt as old as the land itself. And yet, despite his presence, a tension hung in the air, unspoken but tangible.

She was the first to break the silence.

"What did you mean when you said I woke something?"

Lachlan's eyes flicked to hers, assessing. Then he exhaled, turning his gaze toward the rolling hills ahead. "You heard them, didn't you? The whispers."

Evelyn hesitated before nodding. "Yes. I thought I was losing my mind."

"You're not," Lachlan assured her. "But you may wish you were."

A shiver ran down Evelyn's spine. "Why?"

He didn't answer immediately. Instead, he stopped walking, kneeling by a patch of disturbed earth near the path's edge. With a slow, deliberate motion, he brushed his fingers against the dirt.

"This place is old," he murmured. "Older than the stones, older than the names carved into them. The Highlands hold onto their past. Sometimes, they refuse to let it rest."

Evelyn swallowed. "And you think… I disturbed something?"

Lachlan looked up at her then, his blue eyes dark with something unreadable. "I know you did."

A gust of wind rustled the heather, and Evelyn turned, her pulse quickening as a low whisper curled through the air once more. She whipped her head toward Lachlan, searching his face for a reaction, for proof that she wasn't imagining it.

But he had heard it too.

He rose swiftly, his posture tense, his eyes scanning the mist as if expecting something—or someone—to emerge. "We shouldn't linger here."

Evelyn's breath came faster. "Tell me what you know."

Lachlan hesitated, as if weighing the wisdom of his next words. "There's a story," he said at last, his voice quieter now. "A tale told among the old families, passed down for generations. It speaks of a woman… a Sinclair… who vanished into these hills centuries ago."

Evelyn's blood ran cold. "A Sinclair?"

He nodded. "A woman who, like you, heard the whispers. And followed them."

A lump formed in Evelyn's throat. She had expected something eerie, something unsettling—but not this. Not a connection to her own name.

"What happened to her?" she asked, her voice barely above a whisper.

Lachlan's jaw tightened. "No one knows. Some say she was taken by the spirits of the land. Others believe she left willingly, stepping into the past, becoming part of the legend itself."

Evelyn shook her head. "That's just a story."

Lachlan's expression remained unreadable. "Maybe"

The wind picked up again, carrying with it the unmistakable sound of a voice—soft, fragmented, lost to time.

Evelyn's breath caught in her throat as she turned toward the hills, the weight of history pressing down on her chest.

For the first time since she arrived, she wasn't sure if she wanted the answers after all.

Chapter 8: The Unseen Path

The path twisted deeper into the hills, where the mist thickened, muffling sound and sight alike. Evelyn felt a strange pull, as if unseen hands were guiding her forward. Lachlan remained close beside her, his presence a grounding force against the eerie silence that stretched around them.

Her mind churned over what he had told her — the story of the Sinclair woman who had vanished into these very hills centuries ago. Was it truly a tale, or was there something more? The eerie familiarity of her own name tied to the past unsettled her.

"Do you believe she's still here?" Evelyn asked, her voice barely louder than a whisper.

Lachlan hesitated, his gaze fixed ahead. "Not as she was," he said carefully. "But something of her remains."

A shiver ran down Evelyn's spine. "You mean her ghost?"

Lachlan exhaled, considering. "Perhaps. Or perhaps the land simply remembers."

Evelyn opened her mouth to respond, but a sudden shift in the air made her pause. The wind died entirely, and in its absence came something else — a faint hum, distant but growing closer. It wasn't a voice exactly, but it carried an unmistakable human quality, like a lament drifting through time.

She turned sharply toward Lachlan. "You hear that?"

His expression darkened. "Aye."

Without another word, he stepped forward, moving swiftly now. Evelyn hesitated only a moment before following. The deeper they went, the more pronounced the hum became, resolving into what sounded like fragmented words, their meanings lost to the ages.

Then, the path ended abruptly.

Before them lay the remains of an ancient stone circle, its weathered pillars standing sentinel against the mist. Grass and moss had overtaken much of it, but the energy that pulsed through the air was undeniable.

Evelyn's breath caught. "This wasn't on any map."

Lachlan's jaw clenched. "No. It wouldn't be."

A gust of wind rushed through the circle, and with it, the whispers rose — urgent now, insistent. Evelyn felt the pull more strongly than ever, a longing that did not belong to her but demanded to be acknowledged.

And then she saw her.

A figure stood within the circle's heart, barely more than a silhouette in the shifting mist. She wore a gown unlike anything Evelyn had ever seen, its fabric shimmering like the surface of water. And though her face was obscured, Evelyn knew — deep in her bones — that this was the Sinclair woman of legend.

Chapter 9: Threads of Time

The figure in the mist stood impossibly still, as if waiting. Evelyn's breath hitched, her heart hammering against her ribs. She couldn't move, couldn't look away. The whispers that had followed her since she arrived in the Highlands had coalesced into something   tangible — someone tangible.

Lachlan took a careful step forward, his hand subtly shifting toward Evelyn's arm, a silent anchor. "Do you see her?" he asked, voice low but urgent.

Evelyn swallowed hard and nodded. "Yes."

For a moment, neither of them moved. The woman in the circle remained motionless as well, save for the faint billow of her gown in the windless air. Then, as if stirred by some unseen force, she lifted a hand and pointed — directly at Evelyn.

Evelyn's throat went dry. She wanted to step back, to turn away, but the force pulling her forward was too strong. "What does she want?" she whispered.

Lachlan's expression darkened. "Perhaps for you to listen."

Summoning her courage, Evelyn took a step closer. The whispers swelled around her, growing louder, more urgent. As she crossed into the stone circle, the woman's face came into focus. Dark eyes, full of sorrow and knowing, met hers. A sudden, sharp pain lanced through Evelyn's head, and in an instant, she wasn't standing in the misty Highlands anymore.

She was somewhere else.

The world around her shimmered and twisted, resolving into a grand hall lit by torches. The air was thick with the scent of burning wood and damp stone. Men in fine tartans moved through the space, their voices raised in conversation. At the far end of the hall, a man sat on a carved wooden chair—his presence commanding, his gaze fixed on someone kneeling before him.

Evelyn's breath caught. She knew this place.

She was in the past.

A sharp gasp behind her brought her back to the present. Lachlan had caught her just as she wavered on her feet. "Evelyn!" His grip tightened. "What did you see?"

She turned to him, her voice barely above a whisper. "I think… I think I just saw where it began."

The whispers had led her here, and now she had no choice but to follow their story to the end.

Chapter 10: Visions of the Forgotten

The vision lingered at the edges of Evelyn's mind, a dream half-remembered yet vivid enough to leave her shaken. She took a steadying breath, her pulse still racing. The stone circle was silent now, the figure vanished as if she had never been there at all. The weight of the moment pressed down on her, the whispers fading into an eerie hush. The wind stirred the tall grass at her feet, but the air felt different now — charged, as if the land itself was watching.

Lachlan's gaze bore into her, concerned yet unwavering. "Tell me exactly what you saw."

Evelyn swallowed hard, licking her lips as she tried to find the words. "A hall… grand and ancient. Men in tartans, their voices filled with authority. A leader on a throne, his presence commanding, almost regal. And someone kneeling before him, their head bowed as if awaiting judgment." She shook her head, pressing a hand to her temple. "It felt like I was there."

Lachlan exhaled sharply, his jaw tightening. "You saw into the past."

She turned to him, searching his face for any sign of doubt. "That's not possible."

"Yet it happened." He motioned toward the stones. "This place is old magic. It does not follow the rules of the world you know."

Evelyn shivered, wrapping her arms around herself. The reality of what she had seen unsettled her to the core. If she had truly glimpsed the past, what did it mean for her? Why was she the one seeing it?

A gust of wind whipped through the circle, carrying the distant scent of peat and rain. She turned back to the stones, her fingers trailing over the rough surface of one, as if seeking some tangible proof that what had happened was real. Her breath came shallow, heart pounding in her ears.

"I need to know more," she said, her voice steadier now, determination overtaking fear. "Who was the man on the throne? Who was kneeling?"

Lachlan hesitated before nodding. "There's someone who might have answers."

Evelyn's heart skipped. "Who?"

"An elder in the village." Lachlan's tone was grave. "He knows the stories—stories that may help you understand why the past is reaching for you."

Evelyn stared into the mist rolling through the hills, her fingers curling into the fabric of her coat. The past wasn't just calling—it was demanding to be heard. And Evelyn wasn't sure she had a choice but to listen.

Chapter 11: The Keeper of Stories

The walk back to the village was a quiet one. Evelyn's thoughts swirled, replaying the vision over and over. The weight of what she had seen pressed down on her, leaving her breathless. The past was reaching out to her, demanding to be heard, and the whispers in the hills were no longer just a figment of her imagination. They were real. They had always been real.

Lachlan led the way, his long strides steady and sure as they descended the moors. He kept glancing at her, as if gauging her reaction, but she offered no words, no explanations. She was still trying to comprehend it herself.

The village came into view, its stone cottages nestled against the rolling hills, smoke curling lazily from chimneys. The scent of peat and damp earth filled the air. Evelyn exhaled slowly, feeling both comforted and unnerved by the familiarity of it.

"We're nearly there," Lachlan said, breaking the silence. "Old Fergus lives just beyond the square."

Evelyn nodded, though her stomach twisted with uncertainty. Who was this man they were about to meet? Would he believe her? Would he understand what she had seen?

They passed through the village, the cobbled streets damp from the morning mist. Villagers paused to nod at Lachlan, their eyes lingering on Evelyn with quiet curiosity. She could feel their unspoken questions, but she kept her gaze ahead, following Lachlan's lead.

At the edge of the village, a small cottage stood against the backdrop of towering oaks. Smoke drifted from its chimney, and the scent of burning wood mixed with something else — herbs, perhaps, or aged parchment. Lachlan knocked twice on the wooden door before pushing it open.

Inside, the room was dimly lit, warmed by a crackling fire. Shelves lined the walls, overflowing with leather-bound books, scrolls, and jars filled with mysterious contents. A large wooden table sat at the center, covered in aged maps and brittle parchment. An old man hunched over it, his hands deftly tracing the lines of an ancient manuscript. His hair was white as snow, his beard long and braided with beads of polished stone.

"Fergus," Lachlan greeted, his voice carrying a note of respect. "We need your help."

The old man looked up, his eyes sharp and knowing. He studied Evelyn for a long moment, as if seeing beyond the flesh and into something deeper. Then, without a word, he gestured for them to sit.

"You've seen something," he said, his voice low and gravelly. "Haven't ye, lass?"

Evelyn's breath hitched. She had expected to explain, to justify, but Fergus already knew. Her fingers curled in her lap as she nodded.

"I have," she whispered. "And I need to understand why."

Fergus exhaled, rubbing his fingers over the ancient parchment before him. "Then listen well, for the past does not speak to just anyone. It chooses."

Evelyn's pulse quickened. She leaned forward, hanging on to every word. The answers she had been seeking lay just beyond reach, and she was ready to grasp them.

Chapter 12: The Tapestry of Time

The fire crackled, casting flickering shadows along the stone walls of Fergus's cottage. The air was thick with the scent of aged parchment and dried herbs, a mixture both comforting and mysterious. Evelyn sat stiffly in her chair, her hands clasped tightly in her lap as she waited for Fergus to speak.

The old man's gaze remained fixed on her, his pale blue eyes filled with a wisdom that made her skin prickle.

He leaned forward, resting his elbows on the wooden table. "Tell me, lass," he said, his voice a low rumble, "what exactly did ye see?"

Evelyn hesitated, glancing at Lachlan, who gave her a reassuring nod. Drawing in a deep breath, she recounted the vision that had overtaken her at the stone circle — the great hall, the men in tartans, the imposing leader on the throne, and the kneeling figure whose face she had not been able to see. As she spoke, Fergus listened in silence, his fingers tracing patterns on the surface of the table, as if the words themselves carried weight he needed to measure.

When she finished, a long pause stretched between them. Then, Fergus sighed, leaning back in his chair. "You have been shown something rare, lass.

The past does not reveal itself without reason."

Evelyn swallowed, her fingers gripping the fabric of her cloak. "But why me?"

Fergus's eyes softened. "Perhaps because you were meant to see it."

She exhaled sharply, frustration bubbling within her. "That doesn't explain anything."

Fergus chuckled, a deep sound like the rumbling of distant thunder. "The past and present are threads in the same tapestry. Sometimes, those threads become tangled, and those who can see must learn how to unravel them." He gestured to the books lining the walls. "Stories and history are not so different. Both are woven from truth and belief."

Evelyn glanced at Lachlan, searching his expression for any sign of doubt, but he only watched her intently, waiting.

"What do I do now?" she asked finally.

Fergus stood, moving toward a worn wooden chest at the far end of the room. He lifted the lid, rummaging through its contents before pulling out a small leather-bound book. He returned to the table and placed it before her. "Start here."

Evelyn hesitated before picking up the book. The cover was worn, the pages yellowed with age. "What is it?"

"A record," Fergus said simply. "Of those who came before you."

Her breath caught in her throat. She traced her fingers over the leather, feeling the weight of history settle upon her shoulders. Whatever she had been drawn into, it was bigger than she had imagined.

Chapter 13: Whispers in the Wind

The leather-bound book in Evelyn's hands was heavier than its size suggested. The cover, aged and cracked, bore no title, yet she could feel the significance of what lay within its pages. A shiver ran down her spine as she traced the edge with her fingertips.

Fergus watched her carefully, his sharp eyes gauging her reaction. "That book holds truths long buried, lass. But truth is never easy to bear."

Evelyn swallowed, her throat dry. "Who wrote it?"

"A chronicler of old, someone who understood the way the past and present intertwine." Fergus gestured toward the book. "Go on, open it."

With a steadying breath, Evelyn flipped the cover open. The parchment pages were delicate, inscribed with looping script that had faded with time. The first entry was dated centuries ago.

The land remembers what men forget.

The phrase sent a chill through her. She turned the page, scanning the text. It spoke of ancient ties, of bloodlines interwoven with the whispers of the Highlands. Each passage hinted at a legacy tied to the stones, to visions like hers.

Lachlan leaned in, his brow furrowed as he read over her shoulder. "This speaks of the Sinclair line."

Evelyn's breath caught, the weight of the connections pressing so heavily on her chest that she could barely breathe . "My family?"

Fergus nodded gravely. "Aye. The Sinclairs have always been tied to the land in ways most do not understand. It seems you were never meant to stay away."

A gust of wind rattled the cottage walls, as if the very hills were echoing the old man's words. The fire flickered, casting elongated shadows across the room. Evelyn gripped the book tighter, feeling the pull of something far beyond her understanding.

"What does this mean for me?" she whispered.

Fergus exhaled, his gaze distant. "It means the past is not done with ye yet, lass. And neither is the land."

Chapter 14: The Unfolding Threads

Evelyn sat in stunned silence, the fire's glow casting shifting patterns across the pages of the ancient book. The words before her wove a tale she could barely comprehend—of a lineage bound to the Highlands, of voices carried by the wind, whispering truths lost to time.

Lachlan's presence beside her was steadying,his gaze scanning the text with equal intensity. "This cannot be coincidence," he murmured. "Your coming here, the visions—it was all meant to happen."

Evelyn's fingers trembled as she turned the page, revealing an entry more detailed than the others. The script, though faded, remained legible:

One shall return when the hills call her home. She will see what was, what is, and what shall be. The wind will speak her name, and the land shall know her as its own.

She exhaled sharply, her pulse quickening. "This is about me."

Fergus nodded solemnly. "Aye, lass. Ye were never meant to be anywhere else."

A powerful gust of wind howled outside, rattling the shutters as if the hills themselves were responding. The air inside the cottage grew thick with unspoken energy, the very walls seeming to lean in, listening.

Lachlan reached for her hand, his touch grounding her. "We must be careful. If the past is calling you, it is because it has unfinished business."

Evelyn looked between them, determination settling into her bones. "Then we find out what it wants."

With the book in her grasp and the echoes of history whispering in her ears, she knew there was no turning back.

The fire crackled low in the hearth, casting flickering shadows along the stone walls of the cottage. Evelyn stood near the wooden table, hands gripping its edge as she struggled to steady herself. The air between her and Lachlan was thick—charged with an undeniable, unrelenting tension.

She had tried to ignore it, this slow-burning heat that had been building since the moment she first laid eyes on him. But now, in the hush of the evening, with only the fire and the scent of rain-soaked earth lingering in the air, there was no escaping it.

Lachlan moved closer, his broad frame cutting through the dim glow of the firelight. He was all strength and quiet intensity, his dark hair falling in unruly waves past his shoulders, his piercing blue eyes locked onto her as if she were the only thing in existence.

The firelight flickered against the stone walls, casting shadows that danced in rhythm with the quiet crackling of the flames. The room was warm, yet Evelyn couldn't shake the chill that had settled in her bones — not from fear, but from the way Lachlan's gaze held hers, steady and unyielding.

Evelyn's thoughts were tangled in the weight of the revelations they had uncovered. But now, standing still beneath his watchful stare, the air between them felt different. Charged. Unspoken words hummed in the silence, a tension neither of them dared to break.

The air was too heavy, pressing against them like a tidal wave, suffocating in its intensity. They exchanged a glance, and without a word, stepped outside, desperate for the relief of a breath of fresh air.

Chapter 15: Beneath the Starlit Sky

The night was crisp and stretched vast and endless above them, stars scattered across the sky like diamonds against velvet. A cool breeze heavy with the scent of earth and heather whispered through the hills, rustling Evelyn's dark loose curls as she stood at the edge of the clearing, staring out into the darkness.

She could feel Lachlan's presence behind her, strong and unwavering. He had been watching her for a while, letting the silence settle between them like a soft embrace. But the tension, that ever-present fire crackling between them, had grown impossible to ignore.

She turned slowly, finding him standing just a few steps away. The moon cast silver highlights in his dark hair, the strands tousled by the wind. His broad shoulders carried a strength that both reassured and unraveled her. And those eyes—piercing blue, intense, searching—had haunted her dreams long before she had ever set foot in Scotland.

Lachlan took a step closer. "You keep looking at me like you want to run."

Evelyn swallowed, her heart hammering against her ribs. "And if I do?"

A slow, knowing smile curved his lips, but his gaze darkened, his fingers brushing against her jaw, trailing down her neck with a touch so light it made her shiver. "Then tell me, lass — what holds you here?"

Her breath caught. She should turn away, should fight the pull between them. But there was no fighting fate.

"You do."

The words barely left her lips before Lachlan's hands were on her, firm and sure, pulling her against him. A gasp slipped from her mouth as his heat melted into her, searing through every layer that had once kept her guarded.

"Say it again," he whispered, his voice a gravelly demand against her skin.

Evelyn's hands fisted in the fabric of his shirt, anchoring herself to him as her world tilted. Her pulse pounded, a frantic drum against the silence of the night. "You do."

His mouth was on hers before she could take another breath. The kiss was fire and desperation, a claiming, a surrender, an unraveling of everything she thought she knew. Lachlan didn't just kiss her — he consumed her, his hands tracing the curve of her spine, pulling her impossibly close.

She felt the weight of him, the raw strength beneath his touch, the way he held her like he had waited a lifetime for this moment, he devoured her as if he had been starving for this moment just as much as she had. And God help her, she wanted more.

When he finally broke the kiss, his forehead pressed against hers, his breath was ragged. "I've dreamed of you," he confessed, his fingers tangling in her hair. "Long before I ever saw you. Before I even knew your name, I knew you."

Evelyn shivered, not from the cold, but from the truth in his voice. She had dreamed of him too. Those same piercing blue eyes, the touch that felt more familiar than her own skin. It had always been him.

Her fingers traced the sharp lines of his jaw, lingering at his lips before she pulled him down into another kiss—this one slower, deeper, filled with the promise of something neither of them could escape.

Fate had led her here.

And with Lachlan's hands and lips claiming her as his, Evelyn knew one thing for certain—

There was no turning back.

Chapter 16: Secrets Beneath the Surface

The morning light filtered through the cottage window, casting a golden hue over the tangled sheets. Evelyn stirred, her body instinctively seeking the warmth beside her before reality seeped in. Lachlan was already up, standing near the hearth, his back to her, the muscles of his shoulders tense beneath the morning glow.

She watched him for a moment, the events of the night before still vivid in her mind—the way his hands had claimed her, the way his whispered words had melted into her skin. A heat curled low in her stomach, a dangerous longing that she wasn't sure she could push away now that she had tasted what it felt like to be his.

As if sensing her gaze, Lachlan turned. His eyes, sharp and unreadable, met hers. For a moment, neither of them spoke. Then, in a single stride, he was at the edge of the bed, fingers brushing over her bare shoulder.

"I did not want to wake you," he murmured, his voice rough from sleep, yet filled with something deeper—something that sent a shiver down her spine.

Evelyn swallowed, her throat dry. "I wish you had."

A smirk ghosted across his lips before his expression grew serious. "We have little time to linger, lass. There's much to uncover, and I fear the truths waiting beneath the surface will not be kind."

She sat up, the sheets slipping from her skin as she reached for him, fingers curling around his wrist. "Then let's face them together."

Lachlan exhaled slowly before leaning down, pressing a lingering kiss to her forehead. "Aye, together."

The tenderness of the moment shattered as a sharp knock echoed against the door. Evelyn jolted, and Lachlan was instantly on edge, his posture shifting to one of quiet defense. He moved toward the door, hesitating only long enough to shoot her a glance that told her to be ready.

The second the door swung open, Fergus stood there, his face grim. "Ye both need to come. Now."

Evelyn exchanged a look with Lachlan before quickly dressing, the weight of the night before still clinging to her skin, but urgency now pressing in. Whatever awaited them outside was another layer of the mystery unraveling around them—and she had a feeling that this time, they wouldn't escape unscathed.

Lachlan took her hand as they stepped out into the morning light, and as they followed Fergus down the winding path, she couldn't help but feel that everything—her past, her present, and whatever fate had in store—was leading her to this moment.

And she wasn't sure if she was ready for the truth waiting beneath the surface.

Chapter 17: Book of Fate

The cottage was dimly lit, the scent of aged parchment and burning wood filling the air. Evelyn stepped inside, her pulse thrumming in her ears as she took in the surroundings. Lachlan entered behind her, his presence like a steady flame in the encroaching darkness. Fergus shuffled toward a small wooden table, where a stack of worn tomes rested atop the dust-swept surface.

"Ye feel it, don't you?" Fergus said, not looking at her as he ran a gnarled hand over the leather-bound cover of the book. "The pull of the past?"

Evelyn swallowed hard. She did feel it—like an invisible thread winding tighter around her heart. But it wasn't just the past calling to her. It was something more, something deeper.

She glanced at Lachlan. He was watching her, the flickering candlelight casting shadows across his sharp features. His eyes softened as he caught her gaze. He stepped closer, just enough for her to feel the warmth radiating from his body. The space between them was heavy with words unspoken, touches not yet given.

"You don't have to do this alone," he murmured, his voice low and steady.

Something in his words made her breath hitch. She had spent so long carrying her burdens alone that the idea of sharing them, of trusting someone, felt foreign. But Lachlan… he had been there every step of the way. His hand brushed against hers, fingertips lingering, his touch both grounding and electric.

Fergus cleared his throat, drawing her attention back to the present. "This book," he said, tapping the tome, "was written long before your time, before mine. It speaks of a family, marked by the hills, by the whispers."

Evelyn hesitated before stepping forward. The book was ancient, its pages yellowed with age. As her fingers brushed the cover, an unexpected warmth coursed through her veins. She inhaled sharply.

Lachlan reached for her hand again, this time lacing their fingers together. His grip was strong, reassuring, and she let herself lean into it. The way his thumb traced slow circles over her skin sent a shiver down her spine, but it was a warmth that settled deep inside her, a reassurance that she wasn't alone.

"Open it," Fergus urged.

With a deep breath, Evelyn lifted the cover. The scent of time itself seemed to escape from its pages, and the words written in delicate, slanted script sent a chill down her spine:

Evelyn Sinclair, the one who hears the hills.

Her fingers trembled as she traced her name inked upon the page. Her mind raced, searching for an explanation, but there was none — only the undeniable truth before her.

Lachlan's grip on her hand tightened. He stepped even closer, his breath warm against her temple. "This isn't a coincidence," he whispered, his voice tinged with something deeper — awe, reverence... something else entirely.

"No," she murmured. "It's fate."

The air in the room seemed to thicken as the realization settled between them. The past was no longer a distant story; it was alive, breathing, wrapping itself around her like the mist curling through the Highland hills.

And as she stood there, her fingers still entwined with Lachlan's, she knew she had no choice but to follow where it led.

Chapter 18: Unraveling the Threads

The room felt smaller now, the air filled with something more potent than mere revelation. Evelyn's breath came shallow, her heart hammering against her ribs. The weight of the words on the page still sent a tremor through her hands. Her name, etched in a book older than she could comprehend — it was impossible, and yet, undeniable.

Lachlan's presence beside her was a tether, grounding her to the moment. He had not let go of her hand, and as her fingers trembled, he tightened his grip just slightly, a silent reassurance that she wasn't facing this alone. His touch sent ripples of warmth up her arm, and she found herself leaning into it, seeking the comfort he so easily offered.

Fergus watched them with an intensity that unnerved her. "This was written long before your time, before your father's time, before any Sinclair in recent memory," he said, voice heavy with significance. "The hills have been waiting for ye, lass. Ye feel it, don't you?"

Evelyn nodded slowly, unable to deny the strange, unshakable pull she had felt since arriving. It had been there in the rustling winds, in the way the earth seemed to hum beneath her feet, in the way she felt more at home here than anywhere else in the world.

But there was something else, too. Something more immediate. The awareness of Lachlan's proximity, the heat of his body, the way his fingers laced with hers so naturally that it felt as though they had always belonged there. She turned her gaze to him, searching his face.

"Do you believe this?" she asked, voice quieter than she intended.

His jaw tightened for just a second, and then his expression softened. "I believe in what I see, and what I see is you — standing here, holding a book that should not know your name, feeling things you can't explain." He lifted his free hand and traced a gentle line down the side of her face, his touch barely there, yet sending heat cascading through her. "And I believe in this."

Her lips parted slightly, her breath hitching at the intensity of his gaze. The room around them, the pages of history, the weight of Fergus's words—all of it faded beneath the crackling energy between them. He was so close now, the barest tilt of her head would close the distance, would seal the unspoken tension that had been building since the moment she first met him.

For Lachlan, the moment Evelyn had first entered the village, she had disrupted something deep inside him. He had been drawn to her even when he tried to resist it. There was a fire in her, a determination that reminded him of his own past, of the battles he had fought alone. He had learned to build walls, to protect himself from loss, but Evelyn had slipped through the cracks so effortlessly.

Evelyn had spent her life feeling out of place, searching for something she couldn't name. She had built her identity around logic, around pushing away emotions that felt too overwhelming. But standing here, with Lachlan so close, she felt those barriers shaking. She had never been one to believe in fate, yet something about this—about him—made her question everything.

Lachlan's fingers trailed lower, brushing her wrist before wrapping around it, guiding her hand to rest against his chest. She could feel the steady, powerful rhythm of his heartbeat beneath her palm, as if it beat in tandem with her own. He dipped his head slightly, his breath warm against her cheek. "Evelyn," he murmured, her name a whisper that sent a shiver down her spine.

A creak in the wooden floor broke the moment, making her blink rapidly as Fergus cleared his throat. "There's more," he said, though there was a glint of amusement in his eye.

Lachlan exhaled, a smirk ghosting across his lips as he slowly drew back, though his fingers lingered at her waist a moment longer than necessary. His touch was reluctant to leave her, a silent promise hanging between them.

Evelyn forced herself to focus. "Then tell me everything."

Fergus nodded. "Aye, but be warned, lass. Once ye step deeper into this, there's no turning back."

Evelyn squared her shoulders, casting one last glance at Lachlan before turning her attention fully to the book. "Then let's begin."

Chapter 19: The Threads of the Past

The fire crackled in Fergus's hearth, throwing flickering shadows against the stone walls. The scent of burning peat mixed with aged paper, grounding Evelyn as she turned the delicate pages of the book before her. The weight of the past sat heavily on her shoulders, and though she had sought answers, she wasn't sure she was ready for what she would find.

Lachlan sat beside her, his presence steady and unwavering. Every time their hands brushed as they turned a page, a current rippled through her. It was more than attraction—it was an unspoken understanding, a magnetic pull she had never experienced before. He wasn't just watching the words; he was watching her, memorizing every shift in her expression as though deciphering a puzzle only he could solve. His closeness was intoxicating, the heat of his body a quiet promise of something neither of them dared to name yet.

"You were meant to find this," Fergus said, breaking the silence. His gaze, sharp yet kind, settled on Evelyn. "Your name is written in these stories for a reason."

Evelyn swallowed hard. "But why? Why me?"

Fergus leaned back in his chair, exhaling slowly. "Because the past doesn't forget its own."

A shiver ran down her spine, and she turned to Lachlan, searching his face for an answer. He had been her anchor through this storm of revelations, and yet she could feel his own turmoil beneath his calm exterior. She had sensed his walls, the quiet wariness in his eyes that hinted at battles fought long before she had entered his life. And yet, with her, he softened, as if she had cracked something open in him. She wanted to reach for that piece of him, to draw it out and make it hers.

"Lachlan," she murmured, her voice barely above a whisper. "Do you believe in fate?"

He hesitated, his blue eyes darkening as he considered his words. "I believe," he said carefully, "that some things are too coincidental to ignore."

She held his gaze, her pulse quickening. "And us? What do you think this is?"

For a moment, silence stretched between them, thick with unspoken truths. Then, slowly, he reached for her hand, his fingers warm and sure as they laced with hers. His thumb brushed over her skin in a slow, deliberate caress, sending a shiver down her spine. His touch was both grounding and electric, steady yet charged with something deeper.

"I think," he said softly, his voice laced with something almost reverent, "this is something I've been waiting for my whole life."

Her breath caught, her heart hammering against her ribs. The air between them shimmered with possibility, with longing, with the unshakable certainty that whatever this was, it was real. Evelyn had never felt this kind of pull before—the way he steadied her even as he set her world ablaze. He made her feel seen, not as someone lost in her own past, but as a woman stepping into something entirely new.

Fergus cleared his throat, a knowing smile playing at his lips. "You two best be careful. The past has a way of repeating itself."

Evelyn tore her gaze from Lachlan, her skin still tingling from his touch. "What do you mean?"

Fergus tapped a finger against the book. "Keep reading, lass. You'll see soon enough."

Lachlan's grip on her hand tightened, as if he could sense the storm brewing just beyond the horizon. His fingers curled around hers with quiet possession, as though he was making a silent vow.

Whatever lay ahead, they would face it together.

And for the first time in her life, Evelyn wasn't afraid of what came next.

Chapter 20: Fire and Shadows

The walk back to the inn was cloaked in a deep, heavy silence, thick with emotions neither Evelyn nor Lachlan dared to voice aloud. The night air was cool against her skin, but her body burned from the weight of his touch, the lingering press of his fingers against hers. They had already crossed the threshold of hesitation, given in to the heat that had been simmering between them since the moment they met, yet something about this night felt different. As if something was shifting, deepening, threading them even more tightly together.

She had spent so long hiding, burying herself in the safety of solitude, but Lachlan had torn through those walls, piece by piece, until there was nowhere left to retreat. And the terrifying truth? She didn't want to retreat anymore. Not from him.

"Evelyn," Lachlan finally broke the silence as they approached the inn. His voice was quiet, laced with something raw and uncertain. "I need to know what you're thinking."

She turned to face him, her pulse hammering. "I don't know," she admitted. "I should be scared, but I'm not. I should be questioning everything, but all I feel is… this pull."

Lachlan exhaled slowly, as though steadying himself. His fingers brushed along her wrist, barely a touch, but it sent fire rushing through her veins. "This pull," he repeated, his voice husky. "It's not just you."

They had kissed before, had tangled together in the dark, exploring the depths of each other without the need for words. But tonight, something was different. The space between them crackled like a live wire, charged with the undeniable force that had only grown stronger, deeper, impossible to ignore.

Tentatively, she reached up, her fingers tracing the edge of his jaw. He leaned into her touch, just slightly, but it was enough to make her breath hitch. "I don't know what this is," she whispered, "but I don't want to run from it."

Lachlan's hand slid up her arm, slow and reverent, as if she were something fragile and precious. But she wasn't fragile. Not with him. Not anymore. "Then don't," he murmured, his lips hovering just a breath away from hers. "Stay."

The word was a plea, a promise, a tether binding them to something neither fully understood but both desperately wanted. And before she could second-guess herself, before logic could intrude, Evelyn curled her fingers into the fabric of his tunic and pulled him closer.

Their lips met with haste, so electric, so thrilling, a kiss that wasn't just desire, but something deeper. His arms wrapped around her, anchoring her against him, as if he feared she might disappear if he let go. He kissed her as though he could make her feel everything he couldn't yet say, as though he could stitch their souls together with nothing but the press of his lips.

When they finally parted, his forehead rested against hers, their breaths mingling in the cool night air. "Whatever this is, Evelyn... I'm not letting go."

She closed her eyes, her fingers still curled against his chest, feeling the steady, unwavering beat of his heart. The past and the future loomed in the distance, full of uncertainties and unspoken truths.

But for now, in the quiet of the Highland night, there was only them.

Chapter 21: Bound by Fire and Fate

Evelyn awoke to the soft glow of dawn filtering through the window, her body still humming with the warmth of Lachlan's embrace. His arm was draped around her waist, his body a solid, protective presence against her back. The rhythmic rise and fall of his chest against her sent a quiet thrill through her, a reminder of the night before—the whispered promises, the fire between them, the way he had unraveled her so completely yet made her feel whole at the same time.

She shifted slightly, careful not to wake him, but his hold tightened instinctively, drawing her closer. A contented sigh escaped his lips as he buried his face into the crook of her neck, his breath sending shivers down her spine.

"Trying to escape?" His voice was rough with sleep, laced with amusement.

A smile tugged at her lips. "Never."

He pressed a slow, lingering kiss to her shoulder, his lips brushing against her skin like a whispered vow. "Good."

She closed her eyes, letting herself savor the moment, the way his fingers traced lazy circles against her hip, the warmth of his body seeping into hers.

She had never known a peace like this—not just in the safety of his arms, but in the quiet understanding between them, in the way he saw her, truly saw her, and never once turned away.

But reality was never far behind.

The book. The whispers. The danger waiting for them beyond the fragile sanctuary of these walls.

As if sensing the shift in her thoughts, Lachlan pressed his lips to her temple, his voice softer now. "You're thinking too much."

She exhaled a shaky breath. "I can't help it."

He propped himself up on one elbow, his fingers trailing along her jaw, tilting her chin so their eyes met. "Whatever comes next, we face it together."

The word settled deep in her chest. Together. She had spent so long fighting her battles alone, but here was this man—unexpected, unrelenting, and undeniably entwined with her fate.

A soft knock at the door shattered the moment, drawing them both back to reality. Evelyn sighed, already missing his warmth as she sat up. Lachlan groaned, rubbing a hand through his tousled hair. "This better be important."

She shot him a knowing look before crossing the room to open the door. Fergus stood there, his expression unreadable. "It's time," he said simply.

Evelyn's stomach tightened. She had known this moment was coming, but now that it was here, she wasn't sure she was ready. She glanced back at Lachlan, who was already rising from the bed, the softness in his gaze replaced by steely determination. And yet, when he reached for her hand, lacing his fingers through hers, the warmth in his touch told her everything she needed to know.

They would walk into whatever lay ahead together.

And for the first time, she wasn't afraid.

Chapter 22: Through the Veil

The weight of Fergus's words settled heavily on Evelyn's chest as she and Lachlan followed him down the winding stone path. The morning air was thick with mist, clinging to the land like a whisper of things unseen. Every step felt measured, deliberate, as though they were crossing an invisible threshold between past and present.

Lachlan's fingers brushed against hers as they walked, a silent tether between them. His touch sent a slow, burning heat through her veins, steadying and consuming all at once. She glanced up at him, finding his gaze already on her, dark and unreadable. There was something unspoken in his eyes—concern, perhaps, or maybe something deeper, something she wasn't sure she was ready to name. She wanted to ask, to reach for him fully, but the moment passed as Fergus came to a stop before a weathered stone archway, half-consumed by ivy.

"This place," Fergus murmured, running a hand along the ancient carvings, "holds the answers you seek."

Evelyn's breath hitched as the whispers began again, soft and insistent, curling around her mind like unseen tendrils. The book in her satchel seemed to hum against her side, pulsing with an energy she could almost feel beneath her fingertips. She pressed a hand to it, as if to quiet its call, but the pull was undeniable.

Lachlan stepped closer, his heat wrapping around her like a protective shield. "Are you sure you're ready for this?"

She turned to face him, finding comfort in the quiet storm behind his eyes. There was no doubt between them now — only this undeniable force pulling them forward, deeper into each other's lives, deeper into the unknown. Her fingers found his, lacing them together, grounding herself in the feel of him.

"Yes," she breathed.

A flicker of something darkened his gaze, a mixture of pride and desire, and then — before she could process it—he reached for her, his fingers threading through her hair, his lips brushing against her temple in a slow, lingering caress. A promise, unspoken but deeply felt.

"You don't have to face this alone," he murmured against her skin.

A shiver ran down her spine, not from fear, but from the way his voice wrapped around her, low and intimate. She turned her face toward him, their lips mere inches apart, the mist swirling around them as though time itself had paused. His grip on her hand tightened, and she swore she could feel the thunder of his pulse mirroring her own.

"Lachlan—"

The creak of ancient stone cut through the moment, and she jerked her head toward the archway. It had begun to shift, the ivy twisting and retreating as the door groaned open before them, revealing the darkness within.

Lachlan's hand was at her back instantly, steady and warm.

"Together," he said, his voice firm, his promise absolute.

Evelyn swallowed hard and nodded. Whatever lay ahead, they would face it side by side. And for the first time, she wasn't afraid of what she might find in the shadows.

Chapter 23: Echoes in the Dark

Evelyn stepped forward, her breath shallow as the shadows inside the ancient chamber seemed to shift around her. The air was thick, carrying the scent of damp stone and something older, something almost familiar. Lachlan followed closely, his presence a steadying force against the eerie hush of the place. His warmth lingered just behind her, his hand brushing her lower back in an unspoken promise of protection.

Fergus lit a lantern, its flickering glow casting jagged shadows across the walls. Ancient symbols, worn by time, were etched into the stone, spiraling in intricate patterns that seemed to pulse beneath the dim light. Evelyn ran her fingers over them, her touch sending a shiver down her spine.

"These markings…" she murmured. "I've seen them before. In the book."

Fergus nodded. "Aye. This place is tied to yer bloodline, lass. The past lingers here, waiting to be remembered."

A sudden gust of air swept through the chamber, and the whispers began again—stronger this time, more insistent. The sound coiled around her mind, weaving through her thoughts like an unseen force pulling at something deep within her. It wasn't just words now—it was emotion, longing, sorrow. A pulse of energy coursed through her veins, and suddenly, the symbols on the walls glowed faintly, as if responding to her presence.

Lachlan's fingers entwined with hers, his grip firm, grounding her. "I've got you," he murmured against her ear. His breath sent warmth cascading down her spine, chasing away the chill of the chamber's unknown forces.

But his grip tightened when the stone beneath them trembled. Dust cascaded from the ceiling, and the air crackled with unseen power.

"Evelyn," he said, his voice low, urgent. "Something is happening."

She turned her gaze back to the symbols, her heartbeat hammering against her ribs. Images flickered in her mind—flashes of faces she didn't recognize, voices calling a name she had never heard yet somehow knew belonged to her. Her ancestors. Their struggles, their sacrifices, their warnings. The whispers grew urgent, pressing against her skull until she gasped, sinking to her knees.

Lachlan was there in an instant, his arms wrapping around her, pulling her into his chest. His scent—earth and fire, wild and unwavering—wrapped around her like a shield. "Breathe," he whispered, his lips brushing against her temple. "I'm right here. Stay with me."

She clutched at his shirt, her body trembling from the force of the visions crashing through her. The warmth of him, the sheer solidity of him, was the only thing keeping her tethered to the present. He was her anchor in a storm she didn't know how to navigate.

Fergus moved toward them but stopped just short, his face solemn. "It's awakening," he said, barely above a whisper. "The knowledge, the power… it's been waiting for you."

Evelyn sucked in a breath, lifting her gaze to Lachlan's. His thumb brushed her cheek, his eyes dark with something deeper than concern.

"If this is too much—"

"No." She shook her head, her voice steadier now. "I need to know."

She turned back to Fergus, squaring her shoulders even as she remained within the circle of Lachlan's arms. "Tell me everything."

Fergus exhaled, his gaze heavy with the weight of history. "Then listen well, child. The story of yer ancestors is one of power, sacrifice… and a curse that has never been broken."

A chill ran down her spine.

A curse.

The words rang in her mind, intertwining with the whispers. And deep within the chamber's darkness, something shifted.

Lachlan's arms tightened around her, as if he could shield her from whatever was coming. And maybe, just maybe, she could let herself believe that with him by her side, she wouldn't have to face this alone.

Chapter 24: The Weight of the Past

The silence after Fergus's words felt deafening. A curse. The word coiled in Evelyn's mind, heavy and unshakable. She forced herself to stand, her legs unsteady beneath her. Lachlan's steadying hand at her waist kept her grounded, but his touch sent an entirely different kind of tremor through her body.

"A curse?" Evelyn finally managed, her voice tight. "What kind of curse?"

Fergus hesitated, his eyes dark with something unreadable. "One that binds the bloodline. One that does not forgive."

Evelyn's pulse pounded in her ears. She glanced at Lachlan, his jaw set, his expression intense. He wasn't just concerned — he was protective, possessive even, as though the very idea of this curse threatening her made his blood burn.

"How do I break it?" she asked, determination lacing her voice.

Fergus gave a grim smile. "That, lass, is the question yer ancestors have asked for centuries."

A chill ran down her spine. The walls around her seemed to close in, the weight of time pressing down upon her. The flickering lantern cast long shadows, stretching toward her like grasping hands.

Lachlan's voice cut through the suffocating silence. "We need answers, Fergus. Not riddles." His arm tightened around Evelyn's waist, his thumb brushing against the exposed skin at her hip where her tunic had shifted. Even in the midst of this tension, heat curled low in her stomach at his touch.

The old man sighed and gestured to a wooden chest in the corner. "Then take what was left for you."

Evelyn stepped forward hesitantly, reaching for the chest's lid. The wood was cool beneath her fingers, ancient and worn with time. Lachlan remained close behind her, his warmth seeping through her clothes as though he refused to let her face this alone.

As she lifted the lid, the hinges groaned in protest. Inside, wrapped in layers of delicate cloth, was a small leather-bound journal.

She picked it up, her breath catching at the sight of the family crest embossed on the cover. Her hands trembled as she flipped it open, the pages yellowed with age.

The first entry was scrawled in hurried script:

To the one who finds this, know that the sins of the past are never truly buried. We have tried to undo what was done, but time does not erase fate.

Evelyn swallowed hard. "This was meant for me."

Lachlan moved even closer, his chin nearly resting on her shoulder as he read over it with her. "Then let's find out what it has to say." His breath fanned over her skin, sending shivers down her spine for reasons that had nothing to do with the eerie chamber.

Fergus nodded gravely. "Be warned, lass. The truth is never kind."

Evelyn turned her head slightly, her lips dangerously close to Lachlan's. The moment stretched, thick with unspoken emotions, with heat, with something neither of them could ignore any longer. But just as her breath hitched, the lantern's flame flickered wildly, casting the shadows of the past upon the walls.

The moment between them shattered, but the fire remained. And Evelyn knew, no matter what this journal revealed, there was no turning back now—either from the secrets of her past or the man who refused to let her face them alone.

Chapter 25: The Fire Within

Evelyn's fingers trembled as she turned the pages of the ancient journal. The candlelight flickered, casting eerie shadows on the stone walls. Lachlan stood close, his warmth an anchor against the overwhelming tide of history unfolding before her.

June 14, 1673. The curse cannot be undone. I have tried. My father before me tried. It is written in our blood, sealed by an oath we never swore but must bear until time itself ceases. If you are reading this, you must understand — there is no escape.

Evelyn's breath hitched. "They knew. All this time, they knew there was no way out."

Lachlan's jaw tightened, his gaze dark. "Perhaps. Or perhaps they simply never found the way."

She wanted to believe him, to cling to the hope that there was a solution waiting to be uncovered. But as she traced the inked words with her fingertips, the sense of inevitability wrapped around her like a vice.

Fergus cleared his throat, his expression grim. "If this journal holds the truth, then we must face it. Whatever fate has in store, there is no turning back."

Evelyn met Lachlan's gaze, searching for reassurance. He reached for her hand, his grip firm, his thumb brushing over the delicate skin of her wrist. A simple touch, yet it sent a shiver up her spine, heat pooling low in her belly. "We face it together," he murmured, his voice thick with promise.

A gust of wind rushed through the chamber, extinguishing the candle. The darkness swallowed them whole.

Then, a whisper — soft, yet chilling — broke through the silence.

"You were never meant to be here."

Evelyn gasped, her heart hammering in her chest. The voice was neither human nor fully formed, an echo of something ancient, something watching.

Lachlan's grip on her hand tightened. "Who's there?" His voice was sharp, demanding, but the air around them remained still, the only sound the pounding of their own hearts.

Suddenly, the journal's pages began to flip on their own, faster and faster, until they stopped at a new entry. The ink glistened as if freshly written.

To break the chains, one must face the fire.

A sudden force sent the journal flying from Evelyn's hands. It hit the floor with a deafening slam. The ground beneath them rumbled, sending cracks along the stone walls. Fergus stumbled back, his face pale. "This is no ordinary curse."

Lachlan pulled Evelyn against him, his arms wrapping around her protectively. She felt the tension in his muscles, the steady beat of his heart against her back. The scent of him — earth, leather, and something uniquely Lachlan — enveloped her, grounding her as terror threatened to take hold.

Evelyn felt the pull of something unseen, something deep in her bones. She turned slightly in his arms, her hands braced against his chest. "Then we fight," she said, her voice steadier than she felt. "We break it."

The whisper came again, this time with a low, knowing laugh.

"We shall see."

The walls groaned as the temperature dropped, and the room plunged into a darkness thicker than mere absence of light.

Lachlan moved, pressing her closer, his breath warm against her ear. "No matter what comes, I won't let anything happen to you."

Evelyn tipped her head back, her lips a breath away from his. "Then don't let go."

His eyes darkened with something fierce and consuming. "Never."

Then his lips crashed into hers, searing away the cold, the fear, the shadows. And for that brief, stolen moment, the curse was forgotten.

Chapter 26: The Burden of Truth

The darkness swallowed them whole, a thick, suffocating void that pulsed like a living entity, pressing in on every side. Evelyn's breath came in sharp, shallow gasps, her fingers gripping Lachlan's like a lifeline. His warmth was the only thing keeping her tethered to reality as the unseen forces clawed at their souls, whispering promises of doom.

Then, a flicker—a faint ember of light, throbbing like a heartbeat in the distance. It wasn't natural. It called to them, pulling them forward with an unseen force.

Fergus swore under his breath. "We have little time. If the spirits are this restless, they will not let us leave unscathed."

Lachlan's grip on Evelyn's hand tightened, his voice a fierce command. "We move together."

Each step forward was an act of defiance, the air thick with a spectral weight that sent icy fingers tracing down Evelyn's spine. Shadows twisted along the walls, murmuring in a language that sent a primal dread surging through her veins.

Then, she appeared.

A woman, suspended in the mist, her tattered garments billowing as if caught in an unseen storm. Her face was obscured, shifting like smoke, and when she spoke, her voice fractured through time, laced with sorrow and warning.

"You seek what was never meant to be found."

Evelyn swallowed hard. "We seek the truth."

The specter tilted her head, mist unraveling around her like unraveling thread. "Truth is a blade. It cuts both ways."

The ground beneath them trembled, deep cracks splitting through the stone. Fergus held up his lantern, but its glow flickered as if the darkness was devouring it whole.

Lachlan stepped forward, his stance unwavering, his voice steel. "Tell us how to end this."

The spirit raised a spectral hand and pointed directly at Evelyn. "She bears the mark. The burden is hers to carry."

A searing pain erupted on Evelyn's wrist, white-hot and violent. She gasped, staggering as an ancient knot burned into her skin, pulsing with an energy so intense she thought she might shatter. Images slammed into her mind—visions of a past not her own, a promise sealed in blood, a love lost to time's cruel grasp.

Lachlan caught her before she collapsed, his arms a fortress of strength. His breath was warm against her temple, his hold possessive, protective. "Evelyn, stay with me."

Her heart pounded against his chest as she clung to him, her body trembling from the mark's searing heat. His fingers traced her cheek, his touch both grounding and electrifying.

The spirit's voice softened, carrying the weight of centuries. "You are the key, but keys do not choose the doors they unlock."

A thunderous roar tore through the chamber, the walls groaning as the darkness convulsed, recoiling in agony. The distant light wavered — growing dim, slipping beyond reach.

Fergus's voice cut through the chaos. "Decide now! The path forward or the path home?"

Evelyn met Lachlan's gaze. Fire burned in his storm-dark eyes, his grip steady, unwavering. He brushed a strand of hair from her face, his fingers lingering at her jaw, his voice low and resolute. "Whatever happens, I'm with you."

They had come too far. Learned too much. The heat of the mark seared into her very soul, binding her to this fate, to him.

Her pulse hammered as she lifted her chin, resolve hardening like steel.

"We move forward."

The spirit sighed — a sound of relief or finality, Evelyn could not tell. The walls quaked, the darkness screaming as it peeled away, revealing a luminous path stretching into the unknown.

No turning back now.

Chapter 27: The Veil of Secrets

The path before them shimmered with an eerie glow, stretching into the unknown. Each step Evelyn took felt like treading on fragile glass, her pulse hammering as she clutched Lachlan's hand. The heat of his grip steadied her, grounding her in the moment even as the world around them shifted and groaned under unseen forces.

Every breath felt heavier, laden with the weight of unspoken truths and a destiny she barely understood.

Fergus moved ahead, his lantern casting jagged shadows against the walls. His voice was low, tinged with reverence and dread. "This place is older than we thought," he muttered. "It was never meant to be found."

Evelyn swallowed hard. The spectral figure's words still rang in her ears. You are the key, but keys do not choose the doors they unlock. What had she unleashed? What lay waiting in the depths of this ancient ruin? Doubt curled at the edges of her mind, but another force, stronger and more primal, pushed her forward. It was as though the air itself carried the echoes of long-forgotten voices, whispering, calling, urging her onward.

The corridor widened into a vast chamber, its walls carved with symbols that pulsed like a heartbeat.

The air was thick with something unseen, something powerful. Lachlan pulled her closer, his breath warm against her temple. His voice, though steady, carried the barest hint of fear. "Stay close. Whatever happens, don't let go."

A gust of wind howled through the chamber, whipping at their clothes as the floor trembled beneath them. A low, rhythmic thumping echoed from the far end of the chamber, and then —

A door appeared.

It wasn't a normal door, but a shifting mass of silver and shadow, pulsating with an unnatural energy. It seemed to breathe, the very fabric of reality rippling around it. Evelyn's pulse spiked, an odd mixture of terror and longing flooding her veins.

Fergus exhaled sharply. "That's not a door — it's a veil. A passage between worlds."

Lachlan cursed under his breath, his grip tightening. "And what waits on the other side?"

No answer came, only the deep, magnetic pull drawing Evelyn forward. Her mark burned, an undeniable force guiding her toward the shifting threshold. Her heart pounded as she turned to Lachlan, her fingers trembling. "I can feel it calling me. It's like... it's waiting."

Lachlan's jaw clenched, turmoil flashing in his eyes. The firelight flickered against the sharp planes of his face, and for a moment, she saw something raw in his expression—fear, desperation, something unspoken that made her breath hitch. "If you go through, there's no telling what you'll find—or if you'll come back."

Fergus took a step forward, his gaze heavy with the weight of knowledge. "Ye don't have to do this, lass. There's always another way."

But Evelyn knew better. The truth had been pulling her here from the very start. The whispering hills, the ancient book, the visions—they had all led to this moment. There was no running now, no turning back. Whatever lay beyond that veil, it was hers to face.

She turned back to Lachlan, her heart twisting at the unspoken plea in his gaze. He had fought for her, bled for her, stood beside her when no one else had. And now, in the face of the unknown, he was willing to risk everything.

Her fingers tightened around his. "I have to go. I need to know."

His fingers brushed along her jaw, a silent battle raging in his expression. And then, without hesitation, he whispered, "Then I'm going with you."

Before she could protest, before fear could take hold, Lachlan laced his fingers with hers and together, they stepped through the veil.

Darkness swallowed them whole.

Chapter 28: The Abyss Beyond

The moment Evelyn and Lachlan stepped through the veil, the world shattered and reformed around them. A sensation unlike anything she had ever known enveloped her—weightless yet unbearably heavy, like she was suspended between existence and oblivion. Darkness devoured them, but it was not empty. It pulsed. It breathed. It watched.

Evelyn gasped as her feet struck solid ground, the impact jolting through her bones. Around them, the chamber shimmered with an eerie luminescence — walls of obsidian, veined with silver light that pulsed like a heartbeat. The air carried whispers, not just sounds but voices — thousands, maybe more, skimming across her skin, clawing at the edges of her mind.

Lachlan's grip on her hand was iron. "Are you all right?"

Her breath came fast, shallow, her heart hammering in her chest. "Where are we?"

Before he could answer, the shadows in front of them writhed and peeled apart, revealing a figure draped in robes darker than midnight. Not flesh and blood, but something else — something not entirely human.

Their form rippled as if woven from the void itself, and from beneath their hood, twin silver eyes burned like dying stars.

"You have come at last," the figure intoned, their voice threading through Evelyn's bones like smoke and steel.

Evelyn's pulse roared in her ears. "Who are you?"

The figure lifted their head slightly, the glowing eyes searing into her soul. "A guardian. A keeper of what lies beyond. And you, Evelyn Sinclair, are the one who was foretold."

A slow, icy shudder climbed her spine. "Foretold?"

The guardian inclined their head. "You bear the mark—the key to unlocking what has been sealed for centuries. You are the last piece of a prophecy written in blood and bound by fate."

Lachlan's stance shifted, protective, every muscle in his body coiled and ready. "And what, exactly, has been sealed?"

Silence stretched, thick and suffocating. Then, the guardian turned and lifted an arm. The walls trembled in response, shadows slithering like living things as an immense archway materialized before them. Its stone pulsed with an eerie blue glow, veins of power crawling like lightning beneath its surface. Beyond it, veiled in mist and time, lay a city—a city that should not exist. Towers of shimmering black stone reached toward an unseen sky, bridges of light stretched over impossible chasms, and the air itself carried the weight of something ancient… something waiting.

Evelyn's fingers brushed against the mark on her wrist, and the chamber responded. The very air vibrated around her. A force surged through her veins, hot and insistent.

Recognition slammed into her like a tidal wave.

She knew this place.

She had never seen it, and yet—

She had.

A whisper, a memory, a promise sealed in time.

"This…this is why I was called here," she breathed, her voice trembling with something deeper than mere realization. This was not just a destination. It was a reckoning.

Lachlan's jaw clenched, his fingers ghosting over the curve of her palm. His voice was raw, fierce. "If this is her destiny, then I will stand beside her. No matter the cost."

The guardian regarded them with an unreadable expression, then spoke, voice softer but laced with an ominous finality. "Then prepare yourselves. What lies ahead is not merely fate—it is a trial of soul and will. You may enter as one person and leave as another. If you leave at all."

The power in the air thickened, pressing against Evelyn's skin. The weight of choice, of destiny, of something far beyond her understanding, settled over her.

There was no turning back now.

And as her pulse thundered in her ears, she realized — she didn't want to.

Chapter 29: The Threshold of Fate

The air in the chamber thickened, pressing against Evelyn's skin like an unseen force. Every breath felt weighted, as though the very atmosphere carried the echoes of a thousand whispers. The archway they had just passed through pulsed faintly, as if acknowledging their presence, sealing them in this forsaken place.

Mist coiled around their bodies, tendrils curling like spectral fingers against their skin. What lay before them was impossible—an entire city, buried within the mountain's depths, untouched by time yet thrumming with a dormant energy that sent shivers down Evelyn's spine.

Buildings of towering stone stretched into the darkened sky, their surfaces etched with symbols she almost recognized. Some shimmered, their glow pulsating like an ancient heartbeat, reacting to something deep within her. Her fingers twitched, aching to reach out, to trace the markings that seemed to call her name.

Lachlan stood rigid beside her, his grip tightening around her hand. She could feel his pulse beneath his skin, hammering as wildly as her own.

"Have you ever seen anything like this?" she whispered, her voice barely audible over the humming stillness.

Lachlan exhaled sharply, his breath misting in the cold air. "No," he murmured, eyes scanning every corner, every shadow. "But it feels… like a memory I can't quite grasp."

A cold dread twisted in Evelyn's gut. That same pull, that irresistible tug that had drawn her here since the very beginning, now throbbed like a drumbeat in her veins. The closer they stepped into the city, the louder it became, drowning out reason, drowning out fear.

Then, the silence cracked.

A whisper. A footstep.

Evelyn stiffened. Lachlan turned sharply, instinctively shifting his stance, muscles tensed like a coiled spring.

Out of the mist, a figure emerged.

A man—tall, wrapped in flowing dark robes, his features obscured by the low light. But what caught Evelyn's breath in her throat were his eyes.

Silver. Piercing. Alive with knowledge that did not belong to this world.

He did not move like an apparition or an illusion conjured from the city's secrets. No, he was something far worse.

Something real.

"Evelyn Sinclair," he intoned, voice rich and smooth as flowing water. "At last, you have come."

A cold chill slid down her spine. He knew her name.

Her fingers curled into fists, nails digging into her palms. "Who are you?"

The man's lips curved into a slow, knowing smile. "I am the one who has waited." His gaze flickered to

Lachlan, measuring him, dissecting him. "And you… are not the one I expected."

Lachlan bristled, stepping closer to Evelyn, his presence a barrier between her and the stranger. "Who were you expecting?"

The man ignored him. His gaze remained on Evelyn, piercing and unrelenting.

"It does not matter," he said smoothly. "What matters is the choice before you, Evelyn. You stand at the threshold of fate. And the path you take next will determine the shape of everything to come."

The words settled heavily between them, thick with unspoken implications. Evelyn's heart pounded as she stared at the man, at the shifting shadows behind him. The weight of destiny pressed against her chest, suffocating and exhilarating all at once.

The mist swirled again, rising higher, obscuring the city behind them.

Trapping them in the moment of decision.

A deep, resonant sound echoed from the distance, vibrating through the stone beneath their feet. It was not the low hum of the city—it was something else. Something awakening.

The stranger's smile widened, though his eyes darkened. "Time is running short. Choose wisely."

Then, without warning, the shadows behind him exploded outward, tendrils of darkness unfurling like the limbs of some ancient beast. Evelyn barely had time to react before the force of it struck her, pulling her forward. She gasped, stumbling, but Lachlan's grip yanked her back just in time. The darkness coiled and seethed, alive, hungry.

And it was reaching for her.

Lachlan moved swiftly, yanking a torch from the wall, its flame flickering wildly as he swung it toward the writhing mass. The tendrils recoiled with a shriek that wasn't sound but something deeper — something that vibrated in their very souls. Evelyn's mark flared with heat, burning against her skin like a brand.

The stranger laughed softly, watching, waiting.

"This is only the beginning."

Chapter 30: The Shadows Unveiled

The silence between them stretched taut, thick with unspoken truths and an encroaching sense of inevitability. Evelyn felt the weight of the moment pressing against her chest, an invisible force compelling her forward even as a warning whispered through her bones. The air carried the scent of damp earth and something ancient, something primal, curling around her like a phantom's embrace.

The stranger's silver eyes held her captive, their depths unreadable yet strangely familiar, as if they had seen her before—known her before. Behind her, Lachlan was a wall of heat and tension, his breath measured, his body coiled, ready to strike. She could feel him without looking, the raw power simmering beneath his skin. He had become her anchor, his presence both a reassurance and a danger in itself. Because if she fell, she wasn't certain she wouldn't take him with her.

"Who are you?" she asked again, her voice barely above a whisper, but it sliced through the charged air like a blade. Fear would not dictate her path—not now, not when she was on the precipice of understanding what had ensnared her from the moment she set foot in the Highlands.

The man stepped forward, the mist parting for him like a living thing, writhing and swirling as though it feared his touch. "Names are transient," he said smoothly. "But if you must call me something, you may call me Alistair."

The name struck something deep inside her — a ripple in the vast ocean of her past, stirring memories she did not yet own. The very land seemed to recognize it, whispering it back through the wind, through the stones beneath her feet.

Lachlan shifted beside her, a silent threat. "And what is it that you want, Alistair?"

Alistair's gaze flickered between them, assessing, calculating. "I want what was promised," he said simply. "What has been denied me for far too long."

A cold dread coiled in Evelyn's gut. "Promised?"

Alistair's sigh was soft, almost disappointed. "There is a bond, an ancient agreement woven into your bloodline, Evelyn Sinclair. The whispers you hear, the call that brought you here—it is not mere coincidence. It is duty."

Her pulse thundered. "Duty to what?"

He stepped closer, and for a fleeting moment, she swore the very shadows leaned with him, drawn toward his presence like moths to a flame. His voice dropped, reverent, each word threading through her like a spell. "To awaken what has slept beneath these hills for centuries. To restore what was broken."

A shiver crawled down her spine. Lachlan's hand brushed against hers—not an accident, but a deliberate touch, a silent tether pulling her back from the abyss. The warmth of him jolted through her, steadying, grounding. A reminder that she was not alone.

"And if she refuses?" Lachlan's voice was steel, his stance unyielding.

Alistair's smile did not falter, but there was something behind it now, something knowing, something inevitable. "Then the land itself will decide."

The ground rumbled beneath them, a deep, reverberating pulse that sent tremors through her bones. It was not an earthquake, not entirely. It was something older, something alive.

A vision slammed into her—a battlefield swallowed by mist, blood seeping into the heather, hands pressed into the soil in supplication. A promise spoken in a tongue she did not know, yet understood. The feeling of something vast and eternal, wrapping around her like an unseen chain.

She gasped, stumbling back. Lachlan was there, catching her before she could fall. His hands were strong, steady, one cradling her face, forcing her to meet his gaze. Blue eyes stormy with concern, but beneath that — something more. Something deeper. A silent vow, a promise that no matter the choice, he would stand with her.

"Evelyn," he murmured, voice rough, raw. "You don't face this alone."

Tears burned behind her eyes, but she did not let them fall. She had spent so long feeling untethered, lost in the currents of fate. Now, with Lachlan's touch anchoring her, she had never felt more certain.

Alistair watched them, unreadable. "The choice is before you, Evelyn Sinclair."

The land trembled once more, as if awaiting her answer.

Chapter 31: The Choice of Blood

The trembling earth beneath Evelyn's feet sent a shockwave through her bones, but it was the weight of Alistair's words that truly unsettled her. Duty. Promise. Bloodline. Words that carried the weight of generations past, binding her to a fate she had never chosen. The whispers of the hills grew louder, as if they, too, were waiting for her decision.

Lachlan's hand on her face steadied her, his touch warm and grounding in the midst of the chaos. His thumb brushed against her cheekbone, lingering, tracing delicate patterns as though memorizing her. His blue eyes, darkened with something deeper than concern, searched hers. "You don't have to do this alone," he murmured, voice rough with unspoken emotions.

Evelyn swallowed hard, her fingers curling around his wrist, holding him there. His presence, his warmth, it was intoxicating. "I don't even know what 'this' is," she whispered, her breath mingling with his.

Alistair took a slow step forward, his presence an unsettling contrast to the raw honesty between her and Lachlan. "You do know," he countered. "You feel it. The land has already begun to awaken, calling for what was lost. You are the key."

The wind howled through the glen, whipping Evelyn's hair around her face. She wanted to deny it, to argue that she was just a woman who had come to Scotland on a whim. But she couldn't ignore the way the very air seemed to hum with energy around her. Or the way Lachlan's touch grounded her, tethered her to something real in the storm of uncertainty.

"What happens if I refuse?" she asked, her voice barely above a whisper.

Alistair's silver eyes darkened. "Then the balance that has been barely held together for centuries will break. And you will be the one who shattered it."

Lachlan tensed, his body shifting protectively in front of her. His hand slid from her cheek to her waist, fingers pressing into the curve of her hip. "That sounds like a threat."

Alistair's lips curved into a knowing smirk. "It is merely a truth."

Evelyn's pulse pounded as the vision from before—the blood, the ancient hands, the whispers—flooded her mind once more. She gasped, her knees weakening. Lachlan caught her instantly, pulling her against his chest. The scent of him—woodsmoke, the wild scent of the Highlands—wrapped around her senses, lulling her, anchoring her.

She tilted her head up, finding his gaze so close, so intense. "Lachlan, what if I—what if I can't do this?"

His fingers slid up her back, tracing a slow, deliberate path, his touch sending shivers through her. He leaned in, his breath warm against her lips. "Then we'll find another way," he promised, his voice thick, husky. "Together."

A shiver ran down her spine, but it wasn't from fear this time — it was from the quiet intensity in his voice, the conviction in his gaze. He wasn't just saying it. He meant it. And somehow, that gave her strength.

Alistair sighed, almost impatiently. "Decide, Evelyn Sinclair. The land will not wait much longer."

Evelyn exhaled sharply, her grip tightening on Lachlan's shirt. His fingers curled possessively around her waist, anchoring her to him. The wind roared louder, the hills whispering their ancient song, their plea. And as she stood there, caught between the past and the future, between destiny and the fire growing between them, she knew there was only one choice she could make.

She turned to Alistair, her voice clear and unwavering. "Tell me what I need to do."

The air stilled, as if the land itself had been holding its breath.

Lachlan's arms remained around her, his grip firm, protective. His lips brushed against her temple, just once, a silent promise.

And then, everything changed.

Chapter 32: Bound by Fire

The stillness after Evelyn's decision was deafening. The wind that had once howled through the glen now settled, as if the very land acknowledged her choice. Lachlan's fingers pressed possessively against her waist, his grip lingering, firm, grounding her in the storm of what was to come.

Alistair stepped forward, his silver eyes gleaming like tempered steel. "Then it begins."

A deep rumble coursed beneath Evelyn's feet, sending a shiver up her spine. It wasn't just the earth that trembled—she felt it in her bones, a resonance, an awakening. The land. The hills. They had waited for her, and now, they answered her call.

Lachlan didn't let go of her. If anything, his grip tightened, his touch branding her. "Evelyn," he murmured, his voice rough with something unspoken. His forehead brushed against hers, his breath warm, teasing against her lips. "Are you sure?"

Her pulse pounded, her body alive with an awareness that had nothing to do with magic and everything to do with him. She lifted a hand, resting it against his chest, feeling the fierce rhythm of his heart—a beat that matched her own. "I don't think I've ever been more sure of anything."

Something flickered in his eyes — desire, reverence, a barely contained hunger. His other hand traced a slow, deliberate path up her arm, igniting something raw and consuming between them. The space between them crackled, tension stretching like a thread ready to snap. She could feel his restraint, the way his fingers curled slightly against her skin as if resisting the urge to pull her closer, to claim her in the heat of the moment.

Alistair exhaled, the sound edged with impatience. "You'll have time for this later. For now, we must move."

Evelyn forced herself to step back, though the distance felt unbearable, like breaking the pull of gravity. Lachlan's fingers skimmed hers as she pulled away, sending a shiver straight through her core.

The moment shattered as Alistair reached into his coat and withdrew something ancient—an artifact, dark and worn, its surface etched with symbols that pulsed faintly, as though alive beneath his touch. He extended it toward her.

"This," he said, voice weighted with meaning, "is the key to unlocking what was lost. And it will take more than just blood to awaken it."

Evelyn hesitated, breath catching. "More than blood?"

Alistair's gaze flickered to Lachlan. "It will take fire. Strength. And a bond that cannot be broken."

Lachlan stepped forward without hesitation, his presence swallowing the space between them. "Then let's begin."

Alistair moved with practiced precision, lifting his hand. A flame roared to life in his palm, casting flickering shadows over the glen. The air grew thick with the scent of burning wood and something deeper, something ancient. The ritual had begun, and as Evelyn locked eyes with Lachlan, the rest of the world melted away.

This was fate. This was fire. And whatever came next—they would burn for it together.

Chapter 33:
Consumed by Fire

The air between them was charged, thick with something heavier than magic—something ancient, something primal. The moment Alistair stepped away, the world around them seemed to vanish, leaving only the flickering glow of the fire and the deep, dark promise in Lachlan's gaze.

Evelyn's breath came shallow, her pulse hammering as if it knew the precipice she was teetering on. Every part of her was aware of him—the way his fingers twitched at his sides, as if barely containing the urge to reach for her, the muscle that clenched in his jaw, the hunger in his eyes that scorched her more than the flames licking the night air.

She had felt this pull before, answered it in stolen moments, whispered touches, and kisses that had unraveled her. But tonight was different. The air was heavy with something new, something inevitable.

Lachlan stepped closer, the heat of him brushing against her skin like the edge of a flame. His fingers grazed the bare skin of her wrist, tracing upward with deliberate slowness. "We've been dancing around this fire for too long,

Evelyn," he murmured, his voice like a low growl of thunder before the storm. "But there's no turning back now."

Her pulse pounded beneath his fingertips. "I was never going to turn back."

A flicker of something dangerous flashed in his gaze before he crushed his lips against hers, consuming, a demand and a promise all at once. Her hands slid into his hair, anchoring herself to him as the world around them blurred. She knew the shape of him, the taste of him, but tonight he kissed her like he wanted to claim her all over again.

His arms wrapped around her, drawing her impossibly close, until there was no space left between them. The fire crackled beside them, heat curling around their skin, but it was nothing compared to the inferno raging between them.

Lachlan's mouth left a scorching trail along her jaw, down the curve of her throat. "You undo me, Evelyn," he breathed against her skin. "Every damn time."

She arched into him, her breath coming in uneven gasps, her fingers gripping his shirt as if letting go would shatter her. The hunger between them had always been undeniable, but tonight it simmered with something more—a unity, a knowing.

Before either of them could fall completely into the depths of their fire, the earth trembled beneath them. The hills whispered, their voices curling around her like an ancient chant. The magic was stirring, answering them.

Lachlan stiffened, his lips brushing against her temple before he pulled back just enough to look at her, his forehead resting against hers. "It's time."

She nodded, forcing herself to steady her breath, to pull back from the edge of what she wanted and focus on what had to come next. But the heat between them didn't fade — it simmered beneath her skin, a promise that once this was over, nothing would hold them back.

Together, they turned toward the fire, ready to face whatever came next. But even as the magic called, one truth remained — they burned for each other, and nothing, not even fate, could change that.

Chapter 34: The Price of Knowledge

The fire between them still burned in Evelyn's veins, a slow, searing heat that refused to fade. Lachlan's touch lingered on her skin, his breath still mingling with hers, but reality pressed in around them. The ground trembled beneath their feet, the whispers of the hills turning into something more—a warning laced with urgency, curling through the night air like smoke.

Lachlan's hold on her tightened, his body a shield between her and the unseen force creeping toward them. His gaze flickered beyond her, sharp and assessing, his instincts ignited. "Something's coming," he murmured, his voice like steel wrapped in velvet.

Evelyn's fingers brushed along the stubble of his jaw, grounding them both. "Then we face it together," she whispered, the weight of her promise pressing between them.

A dark smile tugged at his lips. "Aye. Together."

The wind howled through the trees, carrying the scent of damp earth and something more — something ancient, something watching. A rustling in the underbrush sent a shiver down Evelyn's spine, and Lachlan shifted, his muscles coiling with barely restrained power.

From the shadows, a figure emerged—cloaked, hooded, their presence exuding an aura of quiet menace. The firelight flickered, casting their gaunt face in sharp relief, deep lines etched by time and knowledge. They stepped forward, their voice a rasp against the night air.

"You have meddled where you should not."

Evelyn's pulse thundered. The book in her satchel felt heavier against her hip, as if the very weight of history pressed against her. She had uncovered something that was never meant to be found. And now, it had drawn her deeper than she could have ever imagined.

Lachlan's stance remained unyielding, his voice edged with defiance. "And who are you to decide that?"

The hooded figure did not look at him. Their gaze was fixed on Evelyn, dark and knowing, piercing through her as though unraveling her very soul. "The past does not belong to you. It does not take kindly to those who would disturb it."

A chill coiled in her bones, but she refused to waver. "Then tell me what I need to know."

A long pause, the fire snapping between them like an unspoken challenge. Then, the figure extended a weathered hand, fingers gnarled like the roots of an ancient tree. "Come. But be warned—knowledge comes with a price, and the truth is not always kind."

Lachlan's fingers brushed hers, a silent vow, a tether anchoring her to him. Whatever lay ahead, she would not walk it alone.

Steeling herself, Evelyn stepped forward, ready to face whatever fate awaited her.

Chapter 35: Inferno of Truth

The night air crackled with an unseen energy, an almost electric charge that made Evelyn's skin prickle. Lachlan's grip on her hand tightened as they stepped deeper into the darkness, following the hooded figure who had promised answers but offered only riddles in return. The world around them seemed to shrink, the trees pressing in, whispering their own secrets, their own warnings.

Evelyn's heart pounded, her pulse syncing with the distant hum of the hills. The moment felt like a thread stretched too tight, ready to snap. She glanced at Lachlan, searching his face for hesitation, but found only determination — fire simmering beneath his stormy gaze. The warmth of his fingers anchoring hers sent a rush of reassurance through her. Whatever lay ahead, they would face it together.

The figure stopped abruptly before a gnarled oak, its roots twisted like grasping fingers. "This place remembers," the voice rasped, ancient and knowing. "It sees all that has come before and all that is yet to be."

Evelyn swallowed hard. "Then tell me," she urged, stepping forward. "What am I meant to do? Why does the past call to me?"

A silence settled, thick and suffocating. The figure raised a skeletal hand, tracing an invisible line in the air. A shudder ran through the ground beneath them, and suddenly the space around them shifted. The night wavered, like ripples in water, and when it cleared—

They were no longer alone.

Figures stood in a circle around them, spectral shapes, their faces blurred yet hauntingly familiar. The past had bled into the present, the weight of history pressing in from all sides.

Lachlan's arm came around her protectively, but Evelyn barely noticed. Her breath hitched as she recognized one of the figures, a woman with the same sharp jawline, the same fire in her eyes.

Her ancestor.

"You have always belonged to this place," the woman whispered. "The blood of the Highlands runs in your veins, binding you to its fate. But fate is not kind, Evelyn. It is a debt that must be paid."

A chill traced down Evelyn's spine, her fingers digging into Lachlan's arm. "Paid how?" she whispered.

The woman's gaze flickered to Lachlan. "By choice."

A breathless pause. The fire that had smoldered between them now burned in Lachlan's eyes, fierce and unwavering. "Then we choose together," he said, voice steady, defiant.

The shadows swirled. The past and future trembled at the precipice of change.

And as Evelyn reached for Lachlan, she knew that whatever price they had to pay—

They would pay it together.

Chapter 36: The Edge of Fate

The world around them seemed to hold its breath, the air thick with an energy that coiled around Evelyn's skin like a living thing. Her pulse roared in her ears, drowning out the distant whispers of the spectral figures who lingered at the edges of the clearing. Lachlan's grip on her wrist was firm, grounding her amidst the storm of emotions threatening to pull her under.

The woman—her ancestor—stepped forward, her presence both commanding and hauntingly familiar. "The debt remains," she intoned, her voice lilting like the wind through the heather. "But fate is no cruel mistress. She gives as much as she takes."

Evelyn's throat tightened. "What does she demand?"

Lachlan's stance shifted, his body an unyielding wall of strength at her side. "We have not ignored the past, nor have we shied away from what we feel," he said, his voice a low, protective rumble that sent shivers down Evelyn's spine. "But we will not be chained to it."

The ancestor's lips curved in the ghost of a smile. "Then you must prove it."

A gust of wind rushed through the clearing, swirling the fallen leaves in an almost deliberate pattern. The great oak's limbs twisted and groaned as though whispering secrets too ancient for words. The spectral figures shimmered, their translucent faces flickering with echoes of love, betrayal, and longing.

Evelyn's breath caught as a new vision enveloped her senses. She saw herself, standing atop these very hills, but the man beside her was different — his face blurred, his presence a mere shadow compared to the solid, living warmth of Lachlan. A sharp pang lanced through her chest. This was not a matter of giving in to desire, for she had already done so. This was a matter of choice, of fate, of binding herself to something deeper than passion.

She turned toward Lachlan, her body already attuned to him, her heart steady in its knowing. His gaze burned into her, fierce and unwavering, a promise of everything they had already begun and everything yet to come. The tension between them wasn't a question of restraint—it was a force, a fire that had been stoked and fed with every touch, every whispered vow, every shared breath.

Without hesitation, she reached for him, her fingers threading through the coarse fabric of his tunic, pulling him closer. His breath hitched, but he didn't resist. Instead, he stepped into her, his hand lifting to cup her jaw, thumb brushing the rapid pulse at her throat. The moment stretched, thick with certainty, until finally —

His lips met hers, not in hesitation or restraint, but in a fierce, knowing possession. The fire between them roared to life, not new but ever-burning, deepening with every kiss, every shared moment. There was no hesitation, no doubt — only the taste of urgency on his tongue, the heat of his body pressed against hers, and the certainty that this was where she was meant to be.

A distant whisper echoed through the clearing — "Choose wisely, Evelyn. The land listens, and the hills remember." But the past was not a chain around her neck — it was a story she would carry forward. And the only thing that mattered now was the man in her arms and the future they would carve together.

Chapter 37: The Binding of Souls

The night wrapped around them like a living thing—thick with the scent of damp earth and heather, charged with something ancient and unseen. Evelyn's body still thrummed with the echoes of Lachlan's touch, her lips tingling from his kiss. There was no uncertainty left between them, no cautious restraint. They had already crossed that threshold, already surrendered to the fire that had been building between them from the moment their fates collided.

Lachlan hadn't moved away. His hands remained firm at her waist, his fingers possessive, like he had no intention of letting go. His breath fanned across her cheek, uneven, heated. He was looking at her the way he always did—like she was something both wild and sacred, something he had no right to claim but every intention of keeping.

"Evelyn," he murmured, her name slipping from his lips in that deep, reverent way that never failed to unravel her.

She let out a shaky breath, her fingers tracing slow, deliberate patterns over the ridges of his chest, feeling the steady, rapid drum of his heart beneath her touch. A slow, knowing smile curled at her lips. "Say it again."

His mouth quirked slightly, but the fire in his gaze didn't waver. "Evelyn."

Something deep inside her clenched. She would never tire of hearing her name like that—from his lips, in his voice, edged with that raw, unspoken promise.

"I don't need fate to tell me where I belong," she whispered, voice steady despite the thunderous rhythm of her pulse. "It's here. With you."

His fingers flexed at her waist, and in the next breath, his mouth was on hers again.

It wasn't hesitation or discovery—it was certainty. A deep, consuming need that had already been ignited, now burning hotter, wilder. Lachlan kissed her like he was branding her with his touch, like he had already memorized her and was simply reaffirming what was already his. Evelyn met him without hesitation, sinking into the heat of him, the strength of him, her body molding against his as though they had always belonged this way.

The land stirred in answer.

A sharp gust of wind howled through the glen, whipping around them like unseen hands reaching, whispering. The air itself pulsed, thick with the weight of something unseen but felt, something woven into the very bones of this place.

The hills remember.

The words threaded through her mind — not as a warning, not as fear, but as truth. She gasped softly, pulling back just enough to meet Lachlan's gaze.

"Do you feel that?" she breathed.

His forehead pressed to hers, his voice low, rough. "Aye."

This was not just between them. The shift, the energy humming in the air—it was something more. Something bigger than them both. The earth beneath them was awake now, watching, listening.

Lachlan's arms tightened around her, anchoring her in the storm. "Whatever comes next," he vowed, his voice steady, unyielding, "we face it together."

She let out a slow breath, her fingers brushing against the rough stubble along his jaw. There was no hesitation, no fear curling in her chest.

Because she had already made her choice. And she would make it again and again.

She was exactly where she was meant to be.

Chapter 38: Shadows Watchers

The night pressed in around them, thick and heavy, wrapping the glen in a silence that felt unnatural. Evelyn's pulse thrummed in her ears as she pulled away from Lachlan, her gaze flickering toward the rolling hills that had once felt like a welcoming embrace. Now, they loomed, their whispers laced with something darker, something foreboding.

Lachlan's grip on her tightened, his fingers pressing into her waist, grounding her. "Do ye hear it?"

She swallowed hard. "Yes. It's different this time."

The wind howled, sharp and unnatural, carrying with it a sound that made her blood run cold. It wasn't the familiar, comforting murmur of the Highlands—it was something else. Low, guttural, ancient. A voice that did not belong to the land but to something buried beneath it. The hills, once whispering of home and comfort, now spoke of something else entirely—warning, danger, perhaps even wrath.

Evelyn's breath hitched. "What is that?"

Lachlan's stance shifted, his body taut with anticipation. "Something that should've stayed buried." His jaw clenched, the muscle ticking.

Before she could press him for answers, the earth trembled beneath them. Not violently, but enough to make Evelyn stumble. Lachlan caught her instantly, pulling her against him. His body was a wall of strength, his breath warm against her temple.

"We need to move." His voice was steady, but there was no mistaking the tension threading through it.

"Move where?" She twisted to meet his gaze, searching for answers in the storm-dark depths of his eyes.

His fingers brushed over hers, lingering for the briefest second. "Somewhere we can control the ground beneath our feet."

The realization settled into her bones. They weren't retreating—they were repositioning. Preparing.

They wound through the ancient pathways, but the land had changed.

The once-familiar route twisted unnaturally, trees looming taller, their skeletal branches clawing at the sky. The air thickened with something unseen yet undeniably present. Shadows flickered unnaturally, shifting like sentient things. Watching. Waiting.

Then, from the darkness, came the first figure.

A shape stood at the crest of the hill, its form barely distinguishable against the night. But its presence was unmistakable. Lachlan stopped short, his grip on Evelyn firm but protective.

The figure did not move, yet Evelyn felt its gaze bore into her, searching, reaching. A flicker of recognition danced at the edges of her mind, a déjà vu that sent a shiver racing down her spine. The way it stood, the way the night bent around it—it was almost human, but something was terribly wrong. The familiarity teased the edge of her memory, slipping away before she could grasp it.

Then, the shadow melted into the mist.

Lachlan exhaled sharply, his free hand trailing along the small of her back. "They're growing stronger."

Evelyn turned to him, determination burning in her chest. "Then we don't let them."

A chill ran through her, but she did not waver. Whatever darkness lurked ahead, she would not run from it. Not when the Highlands had already claimed her. Not when Lachlan stood beside her, unshaken.

Not when she had finally found something worth fighting for.

Chapter 39: The Storm Awakens

The night was thick with tension as Evelyn and Lachlan pushed forward, their footsteps nearly silent against the damp earth. The shadows stretched and curled around them, moving like sentient things, twisting with the wind that carried an eerie hum — a melody that neither belonged to the land nor the living.

Evelyn's skin prickled as she clung to Lachlan's side, her breath shallow but steady. The unsettling presence they had encountered on the hill had not returned, but she could feel it, lingering just beyond her sight. It was watching. Waiting.

Lachlan's grip on her hand tightened as they reached the crest of a hill overlooking the village below. The inn stood in the distance, its windows glowing like embers in the dark. For a brief moment, Evelyn felt the pull of normalcy, the longing for warmth, the illusion of safety.

But that illusion shattered when she looked past the village — toward the distant ruins barely visible in the moonlight. The land beyond was restless, shifting in ways that defied logic, and in the center of it all, a strange, flickering light pulsed like a heartbeat.

Lachlan followed her gaze and exhaled through his nose. "It's worse than I thought."

Evelyn tore her eyes from the ruins and looked at him. "You knew this was coming."

"I suspected," he admitted, his voice edged with regret. "The land holds its secrets close, but there are those who listen. Those who wait."

A chill ran through her. "And now they know I'm here."

Lachlan turned to her fully, his hands framing her face with a gentleness that stood in stark contrast to the storm raging around them. "They always knew, Evelyn. They've been waiting for you to accept it."

She swallowed hard, a deep certainty settling in her bones. She had felt it all along—the pull, the connection—but there was no room left for doubt now. This was happening.

"Then it's time," she murmured, lifting her chin. "No more running."

Lachlan's eyes burned with something fierce and unyielding. "No more running."

A sudden gust of wind howled through the hills, and with it came the echo of distant voices, their tones urgent, almost pleading. Evelyn turned, her pulse hammering. The light beyond the ruins flickered stronger now, pulsing faster, a beacon or a warning—she wasn't sure which.

"We don't have much time," Lachlan murmured, his forehead pressing lightly against hers. "Are ye ready?"

She didn't hesitate. Whatever lay ahead, whatever she was meant to do, she would face it. Not alone. Never alone.

With one last glance at the flickering light in the distance, Evelyn took Lachlan's hand, and together, they stepped into the unknown.

Chapter 40: The Unraveling

The wind howled through the ancient hills, carrying whispers of the past that sent shivers down Evelyn's spine. She tightened her grip on Lachlan's hand as they moved forward, each step heavy with the weight of the unknown. The night pressed in around them, a living, breathing force—watching, waiting.

Lachlan's muscles tensed beneath her touch, his eyes scanning the darkness ahead. "Stay close, lass."

Evelyn nodded, her heart hammering against her ribs. The vision of the shadowy figure still lingered in her mind, its presence unsettling. She had seen it before — somewhere deep in her memories, a warning she hadn't yet deciphered.

As they navigated the winding path, the ground beneath them shifted, the stones slick with unseen moisture. The glen had never felt so foreign, its familiar beauty cloaked in an ominous veil. The hills, which had once whispered secrets of longing and belonging, now murmured with a more sinister intent.

A rustling in the distance made Evelyn pause. Lachlan's grip tightened as he pulled her behind him, his stance protective. A figure emerged from the shadows, its form barely distinguishable against the gloom. Evelyn's breath caught in her throat.

"Who's there?" Lachlan's voice was steady, yet edged with caution.

A low chuckle echoed through the stillness. "You always were the reckless one, Lachlan."

The voice was smooth, laced with an unsettling familiarity. As the figure stepped forward, the dim moonlight revealed a man cloaked in dark fabric, his piercing gaze locking onto Evelyn's. She felt an unexplainable pull, as if she knew him, as if their fates had been entwined long before this moment.

Lachlan's stance remained firm, his expression unreadable. "What do ye want?"

The man's lips curled into a knowing smile. "Only what was set in motion long ago."

Evelyn's stomach knotted. The weight of the past was unraveling before her, a thread pulled loose, threatening to unravel everything she thought she knew. Secrets long buried were beginning to surface, and there was no turning back.

Lachlan exhaled slowly, his fingers brushing against the small of her back. "Whatever claim ye think ye have, it ends here."

The man's smile didn't waver. "Oh, but you don't understand, do you? This was never about you, Lachlan." His gaze flicked to Evelyn. "It was always about her."

A chill settled over her, deep and unrelenting. The whispers in the hills grew louder, weaving into something almost tangible. The truth was clawing its way to the surface, and Evelyn wasn't sure she was ready to face it.

But ready or not, the past had come calling.

Chapter 41: The Truth Revealed

The mist curled low around their feet as Evelyn and Lachlan pressed forward, no longer aimless in their pursuit. The time for running was over. The strange man had vanished into the night before, slipping into the shadows as if he had never been there. But now, his presence was undeniable. They had followed the whispers, the pull of something deeper, and it had led them here — to the heart of the glen where the truth lay waiting.

Lachlan's fingers twitched at his side, his posture rigid. "He's close."

Evelyn swallowed the lump in her throat, scanning the landscape. The hills, so familiar yet so foreign, seemed to pulse with something unseen. Then, a figure emerged once more — not from the shadows this time, but from the very air itself, as if he had been woven from the mist.

The man's cloak billowed around him, his presence commanding yet unnervingly calm. He stood at the crest of the hill, watching them with those same knowing eyes, the flickering torchlight from the distant ruins reflecting in their depths.

"You've finally stopped running," the stranger murmured, his voice a blend of curiosity and amusement. "Good."

Lachlan stepped forward, no longer shielding Evelyn but standing beside her as an equal. "Who are ye?"

The man's lips curled into a smirk, but this time, he did not evade the question. "I am the keeper of oaths, the witness to what was sworn long before either of you took your first breath." His gaze settled on Evelyn. "And I am the one who will reveal what has been hidden from you."

Evelyn felt a shiver run down her spine. "Hidden?"

He inclined his head. "Your blood carries an echo of something ancient. You were drawn here not by chance, but by design."

Lachlan's muscles coiled with tension. "What do ye want with her?"

The man's expression did not change. "Want? No, Lachlan, you misunderstand. This was never about what I want." He turned slightly, looking toward the ruins where the strange pulsing light had grown stronger, flickering like a heartbeat. "This is about what was promised."

A cold dread settled over Evelyn. "Promised by who?"

The man's gaze darkened. "By those who came before you. By the ones who set these events into motion long before your time."

The whispers in the hills grew louder, no longer distant but curling around them like unseen hands. Evelyn's breath hitched. The air itself seemed to shift, thickening with something she could not name.

Lachlan's jaw clenched. "If there was a bargain, we end it here."

The man studied him for a long moment before letting out a slow, almost regretful sigh. "Oh, Lachlan," he said softly. "You still believe you have a choice."

Evelyn's pulse thundered in her ears. She looked toward the ruins, toward the shifting landscape beyond. The truth had been clawing its way to the surface for so long, and now, there was no stopping it.

She turned back to the stranger. "Then show me."

His lips parted, his expression unreadable. And then, with a single nod, he beckoned them forward.

Evelyn took a breath, steadying herself. Whatever lay ahead, whatever truth awaited — she was ready to face it.

Chapter 42: The Reckoning

The weight of the night pressed down upon them as Evelyn and Lachlan stood at the threshold of the unknown. The glen, once familiar, now felt like an entirely different world, twisted by shadows that danced and flickered with unnatural movement. The stranger had disappeared, but his presence lingered, thick in the air, a warning neither of them could ignore.

Evelyn tightened her grip on Lachlan's hand, seeking reassurance in his warmth. "We need answers."

Lachlan nodded, his expression dark. "Aye. And I think I know where to find them."

He led her through the dense woods, his steps determined yet cautious. The air crackled with unseen energy, an oppressive force that threatened to suffocate. It wasn't long before they reached an ancient stone circle, its towering monoliths silhouetted against the moonlight. The moment Evelyn stepped inside, a strange hum resonated through her bones.

"This place..." she whispered, tracing a hand over one of the weathered stones. It was cold—far colder than it should have been.

Lachlan stood beside her, scanning the surroundings. "This is where it all began. The history of these lands, the magic that binds them—it's woven into these stones."

A sudden gust of wind howled through the clearing, carrying with it a whisper—not of the hills, but of something far more ancient. Evelyn turned sharply, her breath catching as the stranger reappeared, his form solidifying from the darkness.

"You seek answers," he said, his voice deep and resonant. "But are you prepared for the truth?"

Lachlan stepped protectively in front of Evelyn. "Enough games. Who are ye?"

The man smiled, but there was no warmth in it. "I am the keeper of what was lost. And you, Lachlan MacKenzie, are bound to the past more than you realize."

Evelyn felt her heart hammer against her ribs. "What does that mean?"

The stranger took a slow step forward. "It means the ghosts of these hills are waking. The past is not just a memory—it's alive, waiting to be reckoned with."

The air grew heavy, thick with unseen forces. The ground trembled beneath their feet as the stones pulsed with an eerie glow. Lachlan's grip on Evelyn tightened. "Then we reckon with it now."

A deep, resonant sound—like the tolling of a bell—echoed through the clearing, vibrating through Evelyn's very core. The shadows that had once seemed formless began to take shape. Figures emerged—specters of the past, their faces eerily familiar.

One stepped forward, his features indistinct but his presence undeniable. Lachlan inhaled sharply, his voice barely above a whisper. "No… it can't be."

Evelyn turned to him, confusion knitting her brow. "Who is he?"

The specter lifted a ghostly hand, pointing straight at Lachlan. "You know me, boy."

Recognition flickered across Lachlan's face, but his expression hardened. "Ye've been dead for centuries."

The figure's translucent lips curled. "And yet, here we are."

Evelyn's blood ran cold. This was not just a reckoning—it was a confrontation with a past that refused to be buried. And whatever truth had been hidden within these hills was about to be unearthed.

Chapter 43: Haunting of the Ancients

Evelyn's breath came in short gasps as she steadied herself against Lachlan. The air crackled, thick with energy, making her skin prickle. The specters that had emerged from the shadows moments before lingered, their forms shifting like mist caught in an unseen wind. They did not attack, did not move closer, but their presence alone was suffocating.

Lachlan's grip on her hand was firm, grounding her. "They're watching us," he murmured. "Waiting."

Evelyn swallowed hard, forcing herself to stand taller. The weight of their gazes pressed against her, like something reaching through time itself. Then, through the swirling figures, another shape materialized — solid, undeniable.

The stranger.

No longer a wisp of mist or a fleeting shadow, he stepped forward with the same quiet authority, his presence cutting through the unnatural haze. His gaze swept over the specters before settling on Evelyn and Lachlan. There was no need to ask who he was — they already knew. And there was no time for riddles.

Lachlan's voice was low, edged with warning. "The reckoning's already begun. If ye have something to tell us, say it now."

The stranger studied them for a long moment before nodding. "The past is unraveling," he said. "And you stand at the center of it."

Evelyn's pulse pounded in her ears. The specters did not fade, did not waver. If anything, they grew more defined, their faces taking shape — faces eerily familiar.

Her breath hitched. "Lachlan," she whispered, her fingers tightening around his. "I know them."

His gaze followed hers, his own features going pale. He saw it too. Among the spectral figures stood men and women dressed in garments of another time — some in the rugged leathers of warriors, others in flowing cloaks embroidered with ancient symbols. And their eyes…their eyes held recognition.

One of them stepped forward, a woman with wild dark curls and piercing green eyes, her translucent form flickering with each movement. "Evelyn," she said, her voice a mere thread of sound. "You've come home."

A shudder ran through Evelyn's spine. "Who are you?"

The woman smiled sadly. "I am what remains." Her gaze flickered to Lachlan. "And so are you."

Lachlan stiffened. "What do ye mean?"

The stranger, standing at the edge of the gathering, finally spoke again. "They are bound to this place. And so are you. Blood calls to blood."

The weight of his words settled like a stone in Evelyn's chest. She could feel it — an invisible thread tying her to this land, to these souls. The specters did not threaten; they beckoned.

The storm overhead rumbled, and the wind howled through the standing stones, carrying voices not entirely of this world. The past was not just whispering anymore.

It was calling them home.

Chapter 44: The Way Forward

The night had grown darker, thick with a weight Evelyn could feel pressing against her chest. The specters had faded into the shadows, but their presence lingered, an unseen force watching, waiting. Lachlan walked beside her, his presence grounding but tense. The man who had haunted the edges of their journey — Alistair — was no longer merely lurking. He was here, a guide in this strange, unraveling fate.

Evelyn swallowed her fear, determined to face whatever truth awaited them. "You wouldn't have shown yourself if it wasn't time," she said, her voice steady despite the hammering of her heart. "What now?"

Alistair stepped closer, his features illuminated by the moonlight. His eyes, deep and unreadable, settled on hers. "You've felt it. Heard it in the whispers of the hills. The land is stirring, lass. It's waking. And you must be ready."

Lachlan's muscles tensed beside her. "Ready for what?"

Alistair's gaze flickered toward him before returning to Evelyn. "For the path ahead. The past is bleeding into the present, and if you don't act, it will consume everything. The ones before you — they tried and failed. You cannot."

Evelyn inhaled sharply. "The specters. Are they—"

"Remnants," Alistair interrupted. "Of what was lost, of what still lingers. They are drawn to the stones, same as you. Same as all of us. And soon, you'll understand why."

Lachlan shifted beside her. "Then we go now."

Alistair's expression was unreadable, but his voice held no hesitation. "Aye. But be warned: once you step inside their circle, there is no leaving unchanged."

Chapter 45: The Fate That Binds

The moment Evelyn's fingers grazed the ancient stone, the world around her shifted. A pulse of energy, both foreign and familiar, rippled through her veins, locking her breath in her throat. The air thickened, pressing in on her like an unseen force, and then—

Flashes of light.

One after another, the visions came. Rapid, consuming, burning themselves into her mind like a brand. She gasped as the first image tore through her consciousness: a younger version of herself standing on the cliffs overlooking the Highlands, her hair whipping in the wind as she reached for someone—Lachlan. He was there, always there, his arms outstretched, but something pulled him away, an unseen force dragging him into the mist.

Another flash.

A battlefield. Blood soaked the grass, the cries of men lost to the wind. Lachlan, dressed in ancient Highland garb, stood amidst the chaos, his eyes wild with fury, searching for something. Searching for her. But Evelyn wasn't there, not yet, not in that time. And then, as if she were floating above the scene, she saw herself, ghostlike, whispering his name through the veil of time. He turned, just for a moment, and then —

Darkness.

The next vision came slower, more deliberate. A stone cottage, its walls worn by the years but sturdy, a fire glowing warmly within. Lachlan was there again, standing in the doorway, his face softened by the firelight. And she — she was in his arms, wrapped in the warmth of him, laughter spilling from her lips as he whispered something against her ear. A life together, whole and unbroken, if only they could claim it.

The images swirled, a tapestry of what was, what could have been, and what might still be. Evelyn's pulse thundered as understanding dawned upon her. She and Lachlan were bound beyond time, their souls tethered across centuries, drawn to each other again and again, only to be ripped apart before they could truly have their moment. Until now.

Evelyn staggered back from the stone, her breath ragged. Lachlan's hands were on her shoulders in an instant, steadying her. "Lass, what did ye see?" His voice was rough, edged with concern, but his touch was grounding, solid.

She turned to him, her chest rising and falling with the weight of what she had witnessed. "Us," she whispered. "We were always meant to find each other, Lachlan. Time has tried to separate us, but it won't win. Not this time."

A flicker of something deep and knowing passed through his stormy eyes. "Aye," he murmured, brushing a stray curl from her face. "Not this time."

The ground beneath them seemed to settle, the magic that had been stirring calming as if acknowledging their resolve. The whispers of the hills softened, their restless energy shifting to something almost reverent. The past no longer held them captive; they had rewritten their fate.

Evelyn reached for Lachlan's hand, their fingers intertwining. "Let's go home," she said, and for the first time in what felt like lifetimes, she truly meant it.

Together, they turned away from the standing stones, leaving the echoes of their past behind them. The future was theirs to claim.

Chapter 46: A Fate Sealed

The glen held its breath. The wind no longer carried warnings, only the final echoes of a destiny fulfilled. The specters that had once loomed in the shadows had faded, retreating into the past where they belonged. And Evelyn—no longer a wanderer lost in the threads of time—stood firm, her soul anchored at last.

Beside her, Lachlan was more than flesh and blood; he was history made real, a love story written in the very bones of the land. Every trial they had faced, every whispered secret carried on the Highland winds, had led to this. There was no more running, no more questioning.

"This is where I belong," Evelyn said, her voice steady, her heart unshaken.

Lachlan's fingers tightened around hers, his storm-dark eyes ablaze with something deeper than mere certainty—recognition. "Aye, lass. And I have waited for ye in every lifetime."

A gust of wind rushed through the valley, not cold, but warm, embracing them as though the land itself acknowledged their choice. The voices of the past did not wail or linger.

Instead, they hummed—soft, reverent, content.

Alistair stepped forward, no longer an enigma lurking in the shadows of their journey. He was not just a guardian of fate, but a witness. "The cycle is complete," he murmured, the weight of ages in his tone. "The Highlands remember, and now, so do you."

Something inside Evelyn shifted— a final piece sliding into place. She had spent so much of her life tethered to uncertainty, caught between longing and fear. But this land had never forgotten her. And neither had he.

Lachlan reached up, brushing a stray curl from her face, reverence in his touch. "What happens now?"

She smiled, the answer clear. "Now, we live."

The sun dipped lower, setting the hills ablaze in gold and crimson, as if the very sky bore witness to the promise they made in that moment. Hand in hand, they stepped forward—not just into the future, but into the life that had always waited for them.

And as they walked away from the standing stones, the Highlands whispered one last time—not in warning, but in blessing.

Epilogue

The hills whispered still, but now their voices were soft, murmuring lullabies in the Highland winds. The morning light spilled across the valley, bathing the land in hues of gold and amber. Evelyn stood at the crest of a hill, the same one where she had once felt lost, uncertain of the path ahead. Now, she stood with confidence, the weight of her past lifted, replaced by the warmth of something new—something lasting.

Lachlan approached from behind, his arms circling her waist as he pressed a kiss to the side of her neck. "Ye look at home here, lass."

She leaned into him, tilting her head slightly to catch his gaze. "Because I am."

It had been months since they had faced the darkness that had threatened to consume them, yet in its wake, they had found a new beginning. With the echoes of the past laid to rest, they had turned their focus to the future—one they would build together, hand in hand.

The old stone cottage nestled at the edge of the hills had become their sanctuary. It had taken work—long days of rebuilding, of mending what had been forgotten, but every stone they set in place, every beam they repaired, felt like restoring more than just a home. It was restoring them, grounding them in something real, something that belonged to them alone.

Inside, the hearth burned bright, the scent of fresh bread and lavender filling the air. Evelyn had found peace in the simple pleasures—tending to the garden, helping the village heal from the shadows that had once plagued them, learning the rhythms of life in the Highlands. The once unfamiliar land had become hers, its secrets unfolding before her like a well-worn story, one she was now part of.

Lachlan had taken up work with the village blacksmith, his skill and strength proving invaluable. But more than that, he had become a cornerstone of the community, a man the villagers trusted and respected. They no longer looked at him with whispers of suspicion; instead, they greeted him with nods of gratitude, with smiles of kinship. And at the end of each day, he returned to her, to their home, to the life they had chosen.

Evelyn turned in his arms, her hands resting against his chest. "Do you ever wonder?" she asked softly. "What would have happened if I had never come here?"

Lachlan smiled, tucking a stray lock of hair behind her ear. "Aye, but I dinna think I would've truly lived without ye." His voice was steady, reverent. "Whatever called ye here, it was always meant to be."

She exhaled, a slow, contented sigh. The hills had called her, whispered to her, and she had answered. In doing so, she had found something she hadn't even known she was searching for — not just love, but belonging.

A soft breeze rustled through the heather, carrying with it the faintest echo of the past. But Evelyn no longer feared the whispers. They were not ghosts or warnings anymore. They were simply part of the land of the life she had embraced.

She reached up, cupping Lachlan's face as she kissed him, sealing the promise they had made to each other.

Together, they had faced the past. Together, they had forged a future.

And together, they would live – here, where the hills whispered only of love and home.

About the Author

Morgan is an author, entrepreneur, and homesteader living on their family farm in Manitoba, Canada with her husband, two children, and a variety of animals.

A retired veterinary technician, Morgan has transitioned into a creative life filled with farming, entrepreneurial ventures, and storytelling.

In addition to her romance novels, she has written Goat Keeping 101 and The Art of Goat Milk Soap Making.

Morgan enjoys exploring creative outlets and finding inspiration in everyday moments. With lots more books in the works across various genres, Morgan is always seeking new ways to share stories and knowledge.

When she's not writing or running her business', she can be found spending time with her family, farming, or tending to her garden.